November

Jackie Clark

Wendülow Publishing

Published by: Wendiilou Publishing
Wendy Brown

Cover design: Wendy Brown and Jackie Clark
Author photo credit: Jayde Lee Photography, Blayney

For more copies, contact the publisher c/-
212 Glenburnie Rd
Rob Roy NSW 2360
wendiiloupublishing@gmail.com
0468 998 268

Please note: This book haws been written and published in Australia, and as such, Australian spelling conventions have been used throughout.

As Australians we have a unique vernacular, and so, we have included a glossary at the end of this book of words and terms you may not be familiar with.

To my cousin Jennie.

A lover of rural romance titles and the first one to ever read *November*.

Thank you for encouraging me to write.

15/01/1974 - 08/01/2021

November

Chapter 1

The rain had eased overnight, and a warm glow of sunlight broke through the clouds to unveil the morning. The land always looked greener after the rain. The fog hanging gently in the cool, early morning air as Claire Gannon drove through her hometown, was slowly lifting. She pulled her small blue sedan onto the side of the road near the gate to the property. The name of the farm, "NOVEMBER" was heavily chiselled into a fallen tree trunk beside a large cattle grid.

It had been ten years since she left the day after her mother's funeral. She had received a call a week ago from her sister, Amy, telling her that Dad was dying.

After days of staring at the walls of her apartment feeling numb, Claire knew in her heart it was time to come home. She had been on the road nearly three days and it was a relief to finally see the gate to her childhood home. A slight smell of lavender lingered in the air as she stared up toward the house, the relief of being here, mixed with her anxiety, was a weight that sat heavy on her chest as she turned her car slowly up the drive.

The trees lining the road had grown high, almost seeming to brush the clouds in puffs of deep multicolour leaves. The heavy timber fencing was now painted white, and the Black Angus cows raised their heads curiously to watch her pass. The paddocks were a beautiful green, and with barely any breeze, seemed calm. She took the last turn heading towards the giant gumtrees that stood grandly on either side of the drive like ancient columns.

November spanned 50,000 acres and fronted the Burgundy River in Southern Victoria; the main homestead was a 300-year-old beige sandstone manor just like something from a Jane Austen novel. Dark green vines climbed the walls to weave through the wrought iron balconies.

As children, Claire and her sister, Amy, had played hide and seek in the sprawling homestead. Using the secret door hidden in her father's office wall that led up a winding staircase to the attic, they'd dressed in olden day bed-sheet dresses pretending to be princesses waiting for a dashing Prince Charming.

Claire missed the easiness of those days where nothing mattered except having fun. She pulled the car between the two enormous gumtrees that guarded the way and opened the car door, breathing in deeply to fill her lungs with the fresh, clean eucalyptus-infused air.

She was home and it was good, but terrifying.

A deep, husky bark came from the porch, the grey faced, chubby black Labrador came limping slowly down the stairs trying his hardest to sound intimidating.

"Hello, Bobby", she said to the half blind dog, his tail wagging furiously when he recognised her. He slumped down at her feet, rolling onto his back for a belly rub, she tiptoed up the front stairs, knocking on the door before she slowly pushed it open.

"Hello? Her heart raced, and her hands shook with nerves. It had been so long since she was home.

"Just a minute" a woman's voice called from the kitchen. Claire's skin prickled with goosebumps.

Michelle came into the hall, her mouth wide open in shock as she saw Claire standing shyly in the doorway. The larger-than-life housekeeper let out a loud shriek and threw her arms around Claire.

"I'm so glad you have come home, love", Michelle dug into her apron pocket for a neatly pressed, white hanky. The housekeeper was close to sixty and had no children of her own. She'd mothered Claire and Amy as though they were her own daughters. Housekeeper, cook, cleaner, counsellor, taxi service, she was a round hipped lady and always wore a white lace-edged apron. Claire couldn't imagine growing up without her there.

"You must be exhausted. Come in and I'll make you a nice cup of tea." Michelle led her into the sweet-smelling kitchen.

Claire sat on the stool at the end of the bench and looked around the room. Everything was as she remembered it. The softly painted, peach-coloured walls were dotted with rustic knick knacks: wire photo frames with dried flowers stuck to them and the metal chicken statues still lined the mantle above the fireplace.

Michelle poured Claire a cup of tea from the same red knitted-tea-cosy covered teapot from her childhood. She had grown up knowing anything could be fixed with a cup of tea and, as she took a sip, warmth filled her.

"This is a surprise, if I had known you were coming home, I'd have planned a roast dinner," Michelle scolded, resting her hands on her hips.

"Amy rang me last week about Dad," Claire said quietly.

"Ah yes, it was quite a shock to us all. He is doing okay though. Surgery may be an option after chemo, hopefully that will give us a bit more time." Michelle sighed, offering Claire a biscuit from a square, silver tin.

"I am sure when he sees you, my dear, he will have a smile as wide as an ocean. He talks about you all the time, every time he speaks to you on the phone, we all get the updates."

Claire smiled, dunking her biscuit into her tea, and shoving it in her mouth before the soggy end fell into the cup.

"Truthfully, I didn't think you would ever come home, love".

"I wasn't sure I'd come either," Claire sighed.

"You're always welcome. You know this is your home, Claire." Her smile was soft as she continued to look at Claire intently. "Stuart still works here, you know."

The lump solidified in Claire's throat at the mention of his name, even after ten years away.

"I'm not sure that he will want to know me now, after all this time". Claire mumbled.

The kitchen door swung open, and a screech echoed through the room as a figure seemed to almost fly through the air.

"I can't believe it." Amy wrapped her arms around Claire. "I've missed you so much".

They held each other for a while before wiping away their tears. Michelle slid a freshly poured cup of tea across the bench to Amy as she stuffed the used tissue into her jeans pocket.

"Come on," Amy picked up her cup and took Claire's hand, leading her outside onto the porch.

Amy was twenty, ten years younger than Claire. It had been hard leaving her ten-year-old sister at home, but Claire had hoped that one day she would understand. Amy had spent many school holidays with Claire in Perth over the past years.

They sat on the porch and talked for ages. Dad had been diagnosed with terminal lung cancer two months ago and swore black and blue that he was fine, despite being given only eighteen months to live. He still was 'boss' at *November* and was not going to relinquish that title anytime soon.

"When is he back?" Claire asked.

"About four usually, he hasn't let go of the place, still drives tractors and orders everyone around. You know what he is like, come on". Amy stood up with a smile, linking Claire's arm, pulling her up, she led her down the path towards the work sheds with Bobby limping along behind.

The red recycled-brick path led across the lawn, past a large chicken coop to a new picket gate.

A sense of grief tugged at Claire for the little things she had missed over the years. There were two large new work sheds just beyond the house yard. The beige blocks of metal towered high with 4 water tanks on one side.

The first one, a large barn style shed with a loft flat above the main workshop, had two John Deere harvest headers and wire loops of ripper tynes hanging from the walls, the second, smaller one was more of a mechanical workshop with a small roller door at the front.

"Claire Gannon, my God!", Billy Wilson had worked on *November* for most of Claire's life and had been like a brother to her and Amy. Wiping the grease off his hands with a rag, Billy threw his arms around Claire squeezing her hard.

"It's good to see you," Claire smiled.

Billy turned the radio down after they followed him into the workshop and introduced Claire to Terry Scott and Jamie Barlow who had joined the ranks since she'd left.

"New workshop looks great, Bill." Claire looked around at the many spare parts and chains hanging from the walls. "Last time I was here, the workshop was a slanted hut that looked like it would blow over at any moment."

Billy smiled at her, "Does your dad know you're here?" Billy asked frowning.

"He will soon enough I guess", Claire shrugged.

Billy had been in love with Claire once, in a drunken state one night he had picked up the courage to confess his feelings. As he'd leaned in to kiss her, he'd fallen into a bougainvillea bush and ended up covered in scratches for days from the giant thorns.

"How has he been?" Claire asked quietly.

"The usual, not much has changed, he still yells orders at everyone," Billy huffed. "Stuart goes with him most of the time now, as much as your dad complains." He rolled his eyes.

Claire's stomach knotted tightly as a soft rumble got louder and louder by the moment.

"That will be them now," Terry said, throwing his oil rag back onto the tray of the ute he had been working on.

"Them?" Claire asked looking at Amy with a wary look on her face.

"Your dad and Stuart," Terry advised.

Claire's heart almost stopped beating for a moment. Stuart was Dad's best mate and had been at *November* as manager for most of her life. Stuart was 46 and like an uncle to her growing up. Stuart had realized his feelings for Claire were far more intense at Claire's 21st birthday but due to the age gap of 16 years, felt it was best to not say anything and kept it a secret, which he managed for years. When her mother died and she decided to leave, he risked it all and confessed his feelings to her.

They'd had a brief long-distance relationship until Stuart called it off a few months after she'd left, it was too hard to get to know each other when they were thousands of kilometres apart. In reality, he knew she was probably never going to come home.

The diesel engine came to a stop in front of the open roller door and Claire's stomach churned when a door slammed.

She walked slowly outside behind Amy as she watched her dad sift through a toolbox on the back of the ute. Stuart looked up as he climbed out of the cab and stood staring at her in disbelief. She looked carefully at him. He didn't have a beard last time she saw him, and she could see how tired he looked now.

"Well shit, I never thought I'd see the day", he muttered sourly.

Dad turned and dropped the hammer in shock when Stuart spoke.

Claire walked towards her father, her bottom lip quivering like a child. Her father didn't speak a single word. He reached out, took her in his arms and held her tightly. Claire couldn't hold it any longer and sobs finally took her as she buried her face deep into his chest. Stuart disappeared into the shed, kicking a stack of tyres along the way.

Nothing in the past ten years away felt as wonderful and comforting as having her dad's arms around her.

Amy wrapped her arms around them both.

Claire lay in bed that night with her heart feeling full. She was happy to be home, but guilt was mixed in with the happiness. Stuart was on the edge of her thoughts. Claire wondered how long it really had been like this before Amy called her to come home, how long had Stuart been babysitting Dad in the daily work? How much had the burden of looking out for Dad as well as managing the farm been for him? She could see the aged and tired look he had that afternoon.

Claire knew that she left for her own reasons, back then she was the only one she was thinking about, but a part of her now wished she had not been so selfish. She wasted five years backpacking through America finding casual work to take her on to the next adventure, Mexico, Brazil, and back home to far North Queensland before settling in Perth. Finding a job at a restaurant and renting a small apartment overlooking the beach, she started to settle down into a routine, to stop running away and give herself time to grieve.

There was a lot of work to do around the farm, she had to make an effort to get involved and try to earn back the right to be there. The guilt she was feeling was getting deeper the more she thought about it.

She woke to a beautiful morning and helped around the house. Taking the food scraps down to the new chook pen later in the day, she went in like a boss, fighting her way past Cackleberry, the big black rooster. She collected fifteen eggs from seventeen ladies, one gold and black chook took a liking to her and let her pick her up and stroke her feathers.

Sitting on the floor of the chook pen, patting the chicken, a flicker of light caught her eye, through the wire, out in the paddock. She stood slowly, brushing herself off and snuck back through the gate without disturbing that damn menacing rooster.

A gentle scent of lavender drifted through the air as she looked across the grassy paddock where the top of her Mum's headstone was lit by a shaft of sunlight. Walking down the yard, Claire stood at the picket gate at the far end of the verandah for quite some time before finally lifting the latch.

Stepping into the soft lawn, she gently placed each foot quietly onto the smooth stepping stones, one after another, counting 27, 28, 29, 30 before they stopped. Standing on the last stone at the end of the path her gaze ran along the circle of small white pebbles that surrounded her. Her Mum's headstone was tall and made of black marble with white lettering. This was the first time Claire had been to visit her grave, she couldn't speak, couldn't cry, she just stood silently reading the words on the headstone.

A Mother's Love,

like an imperishable sun,

cannot go out.

KAREN GANNON

Sunrise 12/5/1960

Sunset 14/7/2010

Mum used to tell them that quote when they were little, and it was written above her name right where it belonged.

"I, you, like an imperishable sun", she would always say it when she left the house or said goodnight. It was a strange quirk her mother had, she would point to herself, then to them when she said it, it was their special way of saying, I love you.

They had even pointed to one another without speaking, saying the words in their mind. That fateful afternoon, before she left for town, was the last time Claire would ever hear her say it. Karen had been going to work earlier than usual to cover another girl's shift; it was raining heavily when her car was struck head on by a year 12 student named Eddie Vanstone; he had lost control in the treacherous conditions. Claire remembered Dad's guttural cry like it was yesterday. Part of her heart was still broken. Four days later, when Dad had to decide it was time to turn off her life support and let her go, she wasn't sure the devastating ache that engulfed her entire body would ever subside. It was no one's fault, the police ruled it as a horrific accident but Claire still blamed Eddie.

She was sitting quietly in the sunlight when she heard her dad's footsteps behind her. Davis took a seat beside his daughter on the pebbles. Claire smiled and rested her head on his shoulder and sighed as every inch of her body pained.

"I can feel her sitting here with you, can't you smell that, that's her I'm sure of it," he whispered as a fresh lavender scent filled the air.

"I feel like a stranger, Daddy," she whispered as a tear fell onto his shirt.

Dad didn't say anything. He sat there, put his arms around her as she cried. It had been years building up to the point now that she couldn't hide it.

"You are not a stranger here, Claire, everyone is happy to have you home.". At the end of the day, Claire didn't know what to expect coming home; she had feelings resurfacing that she had put away for years and, instead of running, she had no choice now but to face the death of her mother and her feelings for Stuart, and she had no idea where to start.

Chapter 2

Claire drove Dad into town early one morning, a few weeks later. Davis sat quietly in the passenger seat pulling the string nervously attached to the bottom of his coat.

"You okay?" she asked.

"I'm fine". Clearly, he didn't feel up to talking.

Claire insisted on going in with him for his second chemo treatment, despite Davis detesting the idea all morning till he got in the car.

Davis had done the first one alone, he just wanted to do his treatments without people fussing over him.

"You don't need to come in with me, Claire,". With a strained look and a sigh, she tapped his knee.

"Dad, if Mum was here, she'd be sitting right here not taking any of your grumbling and I'm not going to either," Claire addressed him firmly.

Dad sat and stared out the window watching the white posts go by, he had finally given up on winning the argument.

Reffshore, her hometown, was still the same. Like any typical rural town, the streets were wide and the old shop facades lining both sides of the main street gave it a heritage look. The Royal Hotel was the only pub in town and was always busy. It was a grand building with federation forest-green tiles on the front walls, beautiful, stained timber, and an old-fashioned verandah.

The weather had grown cold, and the rain was falling heavily as she pulled into the Reffshore District Hospital. Claire dropped Dad off at the main entrance and went to park the car.

Running across the carpark to the main doors, Claire got saturated.

"Come on, Daddy, show me where we are going" she said linking her arm in his, he sighed heavily like a schoolboy on the way to detention.

Davis was a six-foot-tall, heavily built man and someone who didn't share his feelings much, he was very proud and walking into the chemo treatment with her nearly broke his heart.

The nurse called his name, and they were taken into a room with four chairs facing a big set of windows looking out into the gardens. He sat in the beige recliner with his feet up as the nurse covered him in a heated blanket, inserting a canular into the top of his hand and hanging the bag on the IV stand before pushing the buttons to start the treatment. Davis rested his head back and smiled at Claire.

"You happy now?" he barked.

"Can I get you anything, the paper maybe?"

"The paper would be nice, have yourself a coffee while you're there, I'll be here a while."

Smiling at him, Claire had a laugh to herself at him trying to get rid of her. She touched him on the shoulder and kissed his cheek lightly then headed down the hallway to the main foyer of the hospital.

The foyer was tall, with giant red and gold plastic balls hung on the ends of wire strands from the roof. They were quite beautiful and seemed to go in a colourful wave down the room. Ordering herself a coffee, Claire sat with her table number towards the back of the room.

"Claire Gannon!"

She looked up to see a short man in a white doctor's coat.

"Graeme!" she exclaimed. "Wow, look at you, a doctor." He had gone to school with Claire and had been school captain of her year. She never really had much to do with him in primary school but, with her being vice-captain, they spent a lot of time together doing school leadership tasks and running assemblies.

"Do you mind if I join you?" he asked, holding his coffee.

"Of course you can. So, a doctor, of what?" she asked.

"I'm a paediatrician,", Graeme said proudly.

"Wow, that's amazing, married?"

"Would you believe I am still with Lisa; we have been together fifteen years this year," he responded, taking a gulp from his coffee.

"Aw, not many can say they are high school sweethearts, I'm really happy life worked out for you after school". Claire swirled the spoon in her coffee then licked the foam.

"So, what have you doing with yourself all these years?" he asked.

"I went to uni, finished my Bachelor of Education, I never took any fulltime teaching jobs though, rather bounced from job to job, mainly waitressing, travelled a lot overseas, occasional casual relief teaching." She shrugged.

"They need teachers here, you should check out Reffshore Central High, Lisa is the deputy principal, she could point you in the right direction."

"I'm not sure if I am staying yet, Dad's upstairs having his chemo".

"Ah yes, I did hear about your dad, Dr Wong is in charge of oncology here, but be warned, he has terrible bedside manner but is very good at his job." He finished his coffee and stood. "I'd better get back to it, it was nice to see you again, Claire. Please go and see Lisa if you decide to stay, we need dedicated teachers here."

She stood, gave him a light hug and watched him shuffle his way through the tables and chairs and out of sight.

Claire sat and stared out the window. She had always wanted to be a teacher but she let the grief of losing her mother and her hatred for Eddie take over her life in some ways. She had lost all direction over the years, and she didn't live life fully but rather just existed. She had not decided if she wanted to move home permanently. She had the lease for her apartment so was still tied to Perth for now.

Walking back up the stairs to oncology with the paper neatly tucked under her arm, she pondered what had become of her dreams, if she even had the same dreams. She felt more determined than ever to try and reclaim her life.

"Claire Gannon?" A young red-headed nurse was standing in front of her with a set of folders, she had been so lost in her own thoughts that she didn't notice the woman calling her name. "Your dad's session is finished", she chuckled. "He's already left, said to tell you he would wait in the car".

Claire sighed heavily. "Of course, he did."

The young nurse smiled as if reading her mind.

Dad was leaning against the bonnet waiting for her when she got to the car.

"Dad, you should have waited for me to help you", she warned him, frowning.

"I'm fine, I am old enough and ugly enough to take myself places you know, I am not dead yet," he growled, getting into the car and half-slamming the door. "Bloody woman fussing is enough to drive a man mad".

Claire rolled her eyes and sighed. "Men," she muttered softly under her breath.

Davis had dozed off with his head against the headrest and didn't wake while she filled up with fuel.

The drive back home seemed to drag. The trip was quiet with only Dad's window-cracking snore breaking the silence. The rain had eased but the dark grey clouds still hung low in the sky.

Graeme's suggestion had been on her mind ever since she left the hospital. She'd planned to teach high school sport after uni. She loved sport and was very active once playing on local netball and softball teams.

Had she really given up the dreams she wanted so badly ten years ago? She really had lost herself these last years away from home and she wasn't sure she would ever feel completely happy again, strangely enough, she still had a soft spot in her heart for Stuart. He was the only other man whom she loved deep down. He had avoided her for weeks now and it was making her lose focus on why she really came back.

Claire knew she would never get over losing Mum, it was such an empty, hollow void she had deep in her soul, and it was hard to describe the debilitating pain she had in her heart.

Pulling up between the entrance gums, she parked her car on the gravel outside the homestead as Michelle came down the front stairs to greet them.

Davis got out of the car slowly and was feeling like all the energy had been drained from his body. He was a proud man, and he wasn't going to let people see him at his weakest. This time, however, he allowed Claire and Michelle help him at home. He weakly gave in to the women's persistent nagging and went to bed.

Amy had started cleaning up the dishes when Stuart came in with his bowl after eating his meal on the verandah. The mood was very sombre, Stuart stood in the hallway quietly watching the moon through the front door while listening to the conversation.

"How was Dad today?" Amy asked.

"His usual, stubborn, pain-in-the-bum self", Claire snarled, wiping the last of her soup with the bread, passing her bowl to Michelle who was stacking the dishwasher. "I ran into Graeme Donaldson. He is still with Lisa after all this time", she mused.

"Yeah, they got married a few years back, they've been together since the 9th grade", Amy added.

"My husband and I were childhood sweethearts", Michelle said as she put a large wooden tray on the counter. First a dinner plate, followed by a bowl of soup and bread beside it. A knife and fork on one side and a small glass bowl of butter, a pot of salt and pepper on the other.

"I'm not sure he will eat much tonight, but I'll take something up anyway", Michelle gently lifted the tray and headed upstairs. As she passed Stuart in the hall, she turned to him with a meaningful smile. "You should go in and talk to her," then continued up the stairs.

He was hurting, his heart felt like it had fallen out of his chest the day Claire came home. Stuart always thought warmly of her growing up, when he realised his feelings for her had become stronger, he kept it secret for years. Stuart took a deep breath, awkwardly walking back into the kitchen and flicking on the jug to make a coffee. Amy cheekily shoved him, holding out her cup with a smirk.

"Coffee anyone?", she asked as she passed around an old, round biscuit tin.

Claire came over to his side and handed him her cup. She felt his fingers touch her hand as he took the cup from her, he was so close that she could see the grey hairs scattered through his beard. His eyes met hers for a moment before he pulled away, placing her cup down with the others. She wanted to talk to him about everything, but she was scared of opening herself up to him, what if he didn't feel the same anymore? He had practically avoided her since she got home. She felt emotional and tired.

"Graeme suggested I call into Reffshore Central and talk to Lisa about a teaching position there".

Stuart looked up at her in shock, she met his gaze again and he pulled away. The room suddenly seemed to go into slow motion. Stuart's eyes grew wider. Stirring the milk into his coffee, he tried to retain the same level expression while hiding the hot surge of nerves that shot through his stomach.

"A job?" Amy questioned, talking with her mouth full of biscuit. "Are you going to stay?" She swallowed her mouthful, then slugged half of the coffee to wash it down. Claire looked at Amy who seemed to be hanging on her words and waiting for an answer. Still standing beside Stuart, she leant on the bench close enough that she could smell his aftershave.

"I'm thinking 'bout it I guess,". She said, holding her breath as Stuart looked across into her eyes once again. He raised the cup high, drinking the last of his coffee, put the cup in the sink, and quietly left the kitchen. Claire sighed heavily, rubbing her hand over her eyes, and plonked down hard onto the stool.

"He will come round" Amy put her hand on her chest and then to Claire. "I, you".

Claire smiled, "I, you, too".

Claire checked on Dad late that night. He was sleeping. He was losing his hair, not only on his head but his beard also. He seemed to have aged so much since she had been gone, she wondered how long the cancer had been attacking his body before they found the problem. Being a stubborn mule at the best of times, and a typical man, he would have put up with pain and discomfort rather than seeing a doctor. Quietly she walked into the room, put her gloves on and cleaned up the tissues he had beside him on the bed. Carefully packing up the tray with his soup, she noticed that he seemed to have had a bit. She carried the tray into the kitchen and stacked the dishes into the dishwasher and took the bagged tissues outside to the incinerator.

Looking at her phone, she was surprised to find it was nearly 10.30pm. She had several missed calls and a few voice messages. Dialling her voice mail, she listened to the three messages. One from her friend, Pia, checking up on her and two from the real estate letting her know the lease was coming to an end soon and to contact them on this number asap. She hung up the phone, sighing heavily.

Chapter 3

Claire woke early. Her mind was full of questions with no answers, walking down the hall to her father's door she knocked quietly before pushing it open. Michelle was cleaning up the vomit on the side of the bed.

"Let me help you", Claire rushed to her side.

"No, no, I'm fine, love," Michelle smiled looking every bit the nurse matron. "I sent him to have a shower."

Claire nodded, looking wide eyed at the mess on his bed and found herself getting emotional, a tear falling down her cheek.

"He is ok, this is normal for someone who has had chemo, my husband went through it many times before he died", she said with a comforting smile.

"I'm sorry, Michelle", Claire spoke with eyes full of tears.

"Ahhh love, we had 35 years of marriage, I'd not change it, life is tough sometimes", Michelle put all the soiled bed linen in a big basket before remaking the bed with fresh yellow sheets.

"I'm not ready," Claire spluttered as she started to cry. "I don't want to say goodbye to him", she said, trying hard to hold back tears. Michelle smiled and stretched her arms out giving Claire a hug.

"I guess all we can do it try to make the most of every moment, when it's his time there isn't much you, or I, can do about it, we can just be here when he needs us and love him", she comforted softly.

"What would we ever do without you?" Dad stood at the door looking quite pale.

"We would starve," he confirmed as he hobbled into the room. "We would be very lost indeed", he smiled with a heartfelt glance, leaving Michelle blushing. "What you up to miss?" he asked as he got back into bed.

"Ahh, not much, just checking on the patient", Claire said with a smirk.

"I'm very well looked after, thank you", he smugly stated sitting in bed, a chuffed look to his face.

"Try and eat some breakfast", Michelle prompted him to the tray of scrambled eggs and toast. "You should keep eating despite the vomiting", she placed a comforting hand on his knee. "You should start to feel better soon, hopefully", she smiled, pulling his blankets up and handing him a small clear container with his morning medication in it.

Stuart sat in the office working on some paperwork. Claire watched him from the hallway through the stained-glass double doors that led into her father's study.

"Hi," she said, standing at the door.

"Hey Claire", his deep voice rumbled.

"Do you have a minute?" Claire asked, slowly edging through the door. "I think there is something going on with Dad and Michelle." She proclaimed with a confused look.

"They have become quite reliant on each other over the years, Claire", Stuart said without lifting his head from the papers in front of him.

"I feel terrible, if only I had stayed", she mumbled quietly slipping into the chair in front of him.

"I think they would have found each other in the end no matter", looking at her without expression. "That's not all is it? I can see it all over your face" Stuart uttered with some annoyance.

"My lease is up on my apartment soon", she said picking at the studs that lined chair she was sitting in.

"What does that mean for you?" he asked her, playing with his beard.

"I can renew it for another 12 months or I can move out".

"I don't really have all that much stuff so I could have it picked up by a removalist easy enough, I have a friend living there at the moment and I'm sure she would be more than happy to take up the lease herself". She looked up at him for any hint of advice, secretly hoping he would perhaps encourage her to stay.

"What do you want, Claire?" he asked seriously. "At the end of the day, it's your decision, no one can make it for you. You will do what you want anyway, despite hurting those around you". Stuart instantly regretted saying that.

She sighed and rubbed her face with the palm of her hand in frustration, before she could think, her mouth opened and out it came.

"Do you really hate me that much?" She was just as stunned as he was when the words fell out of her mouth, the type of verbal diarrhea that comes out without any thought, and unfortunately for her, her mouth seemed to throw more fuel on the fire, she couldn't stop herself.

"You have not spoken more than 5 words to me in 3 weeks, Stuart, I've been trying to make it right between us, but you won't even give me a chance", She half yelled at him in a teary choking sob. "What do I have to do to make things right? You tell me, come on!"

"Bloody hell, woman", Stuart stood up and leant his hands down on the table right in front of her.

"Claire, you walked out of here that day like the only person that mattered was you. Every one of us was hurting, your sister lost you and a mother, your father lost a wife and a daughter, we all lost a dear friend", He started to choke up. "I can't tell you the number of nights I helped Michelle carry your father up the stairs to bed, he was so drunk he couldn't walk, but you didn't know that 'cause you were not here".

Claire sat back down and stayed very still, quietly staring at the floor.

"I don't hate you; I could never hate you, but you can't come home after 10 years and expect everything to be as it was", he sat down hard in the chair.

"I want to make things better between us, I want to fix it", she declared seriously. "Tell me how to fix it".

He sighed, stood up, put his hat on and walked to the door.

"You want to fix things, right? Don't leave him again".

Chapter 4

Amy and Claire sat together on the white stones sorting through a bag containing packets of seeds. The sun was shining and there was not a cloud in the sky. The girls had decided to make a flower garden around the grave site. Amy had drawn a line in the dirt where she wanted the beds to sit. Back and forth the girls came from the garden shed at the back of the chook pen carrying bricks. By mid-afternoon they had built a raised bed on one side of the headstone. Earlier, Terry had dropped a load of soil near the gate with the loader. Claire pushed the wheelbarrow back and forth tipping the dirt into the beds. The scent of lavender filled the air as they planted a few bulbs and seeds.

"I'm sorry for leaving you after Mum died, I love you so much and I should have been here for you."

Amy stopped and looked at her mother's headstone, trying not to cry. She sprinkled the seeds into the holes and covered them over.

"I should have been here when you got your first boyfriend, your first period even, I can't explain to you why I left".

Amy wiped the tears from her cheeks, touching her chest and then pointing to Claire. "I..You..Like an Imperishable Sun". Claire wrapped her arms around her little sister and they both cried.

"I see him every now and then, Eddie, I mean".

Claire felt a surge of rage through her chest at the mention of his name.

"Don't speak his name around me, Amy".

"You need to talk about him, it was an accident, Claire," Amy begged. Claire pursed her lips tightly and looked away. There is no way she was ready to forgive that man, he killed their mother.

"Just because you can forgive him doesn't mean I have to, to think they accepted him into the Police force is beyond me", Claire huffed.

"I think Mum follows me you know", Amy said. "I smell her. I know it sounds weird, but I do, it's like apples crossed with lavender, not all the time, but every now and then, like I smelt it when we started the garden this morning".

Claire's mind raced through countless memories, taking her back to when she first pulled into *November*, she remembered suddenly smelling lavender but never thought anything of it at the time. Claire stood and walked over to the headstone. Running her fingers across the words.

"What makes you think it's Mum?" Claire asked.

"I spoke to a woman once while I was waiting for Dad at the doctor's, she was telling me that after her husband died, she could sometimes smell his cigarettes and she said it was him saying hello, guess it stuck in my mind after that, it makes me happy to think that she is around me". Amy smiled and moved her hands over the dirt to smooth it free from lumps before picking up the watering can.

"I smelt lavender when I pulled into the drive, the day I came home", Claire whispered to the headstone as she moved her fingers over the white letters. She hung her head, trying not to cry.

Claire, wobbling all over the place, staggered up the path towards the sheds. After a battle with the side door, she fell through as it opened, her hands stopping her fall onto the concrete. She sat in the machinery shed, swigging the vodka strait from the bottle, Bobby sat under a tree watching.

Stuart pulled the ute into the drive and pushed the button to open the roller doors, staring out the windscreen looking quite baffled, he slowly took off his hat. As the door opened higher, he could see her sitting in a stack of tyres with her bum deep in the hole making her legs sit high in the air. He slowly got out of the ute and walked closer to her. She was drunk.

"Hi", she managed to say with a high-pitched croaky voice.

He smiled, smacking the dust off his hat against his leg, walking over to where she was sitting. Her hand was bleeding from when she had fallen through the door.

"Maybe you should let me have that", he said, taking the bottle and putting it on the floor. Taking a hanky from his pocket he took her hand, looked at the grazed skin on her palm before wrapping it up.

"Can we talk?" she slurred awkwardly, trying to get out of the tyres but sinking herself deeper into the hole.

Stuart found himself struggling to look at her and after a few moments of silence he sighed and sat in front of her on an upturned blue milk crate.

"Sure," he said shyly. Clearing her throat like she was about to address the nation, she took a deep breath and tried to open her mouth to talk a few times but couldn't think of how to start. "You know, I've rehearsed this five times today, and now I can't remember what I was going to say first". She wasn't as slurry but was starting to get emotional.

Stuart stroked his beard; it was hard watching her struggle, but he just sat there quietly.

"I guess need to start with how sorry I am for the way I treated you when you came to Perth. I didn't mean it, what I said", she took a deep breath as a tear landed on her cheek.

"That was 9 years ago, Claire, it's ok", he said, quietly trying to shake it off.

"No, it is not ok, I was selfish, and you were right, I couldn't see anyone else's pain but my own. I am sorry for making you feel like I didn't care about you, I did care, I do care". Claire reached for a crinkly rag that was hanging on the toolbox beside the tyre stack.

All the emotions she had felt in the last month since coming back had built to this point, with the aid of half a bottle of Vodka she couldn't stop herself. Stuart felt a lump growing as he listened to her cry but still slur, sniffing and blowing her nose hard with a loud toot into the grease rag leaving black grime all over her face. He smiled, trying not to laugh, she really was a pitiful sight.

"You told me you loved me that day," she sobbed louder. "I didn't handle that because I felt like I was drowning when Mum died". She hung her head; it was getting harder to look at him.

"I couldn't give you my heart because it was broken, I told you I didn't have any feelings for you because I didn't know how to let you love me".

Stuart's top lip quivered; he held back a heavy lump building in his throat. He could see she was genuine in her words but still found himself sitting there, unable to speak. Claire was crying and laughing at the same time as she tried to get down from the tyres sending them flying in every direction as she tumbled onto the floor in front of him.

"I lied when I said I didn't love you".

Stuart stared hard-faced at her. He stood up, pulling her to her feet. She threw her arms around his neck tightly. He held her for what seemed like forever, as he lowered his face to hers, he could feel her teary cheek softly against his. It was intense, and as she let go of him, she was still holding his hand, looking up into his blue eyes.

He broke away from the moment. He felt torn and heartbroken but on the other hand he felt a rush of feelings he had not felt for a long time. Awkward and stumbling his words, he desperately wanted to get out of there, he was sweating and dizzy.

"I need to get a few things done before dark, I'll catch up with you later, ok", he said as he let go of her hand and headed to the door, taking himself away. He felt vulnerable, and he knew if he stayed there, he may not be able to control his emotions. As she watched him climb into the ute and drive away, she slumped onto the floor and cried loudly.

Chapter 5

The happiness Davis felt having both of his girls back under one roof shined brightly through his enormous smile that morning. Since his last chemo treatment, and besides looking a little balder, he felt great.

Terry and Billy had spent the early hours bringing the sheep in from Ruby Row, a collection of paddocks that ran along the eastern side of *November* that was named after the rows of ruby red apple trees scattered along the fence line.

The shearing shed was a buzz of excitement. Amy and Claire roused just like old times as the shearers went through the mob one by one, with 700 to shear, the day was going to be long. It felt so good to be home and life seemed to be normal once again.

Stuart pulled the 4x4 into park in front of the new shearing shed Davis had had built 12 months ago only a small drive from the main house. It was the same beige colour as the work sheds and was beautifully done inside with polished timber floors and shiny steel pens. Davis had been spending a lot of time and money upgrading the sheds and housing which, Stuart suspected, was so it was ready to sell when he died if the girls didn't decide to stay on.

"Hey", he said to Claire as he came up the shearing shed stairs towards her. They had been talking more and more since her drunken episode and each time it was getting a little easier. He even found himself flirting and feeling butterflies again when she was around.

Deep down, she still adored Stuart. He was honest and genuine. She was slowly becoming used to seeing him with a beard, which was nearly down to his waist now, and she couldn't resist giving it a cheeky tug to his surprise when walking past, sending a surge of heat shooting through his stomach.

In a toss of Terry's hands, the sheet of white fleece flew onto the sorting table ready for Claire to pick out any unwanted debris before passing it to Jamie who pushed it down inside the bale bags ready for the machine to press them down tightly. Amy swept the wool away from around the shearer's feet, keeping the area clean. The oils from the sheep wool on the new floorboards had begun leaving a deep stain to the woodgrain under the shearer's feet and a soft feeling on the hands. Michelle came in about midday with three trays of sandwiches and freshly baked scones with jam and cream. She set up an urn on the ute tray for tea and coffee.

"Are you ok?" she asked Davis.

"I'm fine, woman, stop fussing", he said, giving her a cheeky grin, leaving Amy and Claire looking at each other dumbfounded.

Claire sat on a stump in the small pen of orphaned lambs with 2 bottles of milk. The lambs were drinking it fast with noisy slurps while their little tails were jiggling around with pleasure.

"Looks like you never left", Stuart smiled as he leant his elbows on the gate looking down at her.

"I've missed it, I won't lie", she looked up at him with a smile.

"So do you plan on staying?" he asked softly as he knelt down to her level with the wire gate between them.

She looked into his face to see his striking blue eyes were desperately waiting for an answer.

"Truthfully, I have not decided, I thought I'd just see how it went, I guess", she shrugged.

"I've not seen your dad this happy in a long time, it's because of you, you know", he noted, looking over at Davis.

"We have all missed you", he added in a soft whisper.

Claire smiled and found herself staring at him before she broke away from the moment. Stuart stood, adjusting his hat, and looking down at her with a little hurt in his eyes. She could feel her cheeks burning red and kept her head down to try to hide it. The lambs finished the bottles and she stood at the gate with her hand on the latch ready to open it. Stuart lifted his elbows off the top of the gate and stood there looking at her with a blank expression. Looking down at her he couldn't remember ever noticing the light spray of brown freckles that had settled across her nose nor did he ever notice that her long, naturally curly hair smelt of strawberries.

He'd been a part of the family for most of her life and seeing her again, working the farm like old times had changed nothing for him. She still made him weak at the knees, it took every ounce of him to hold his composure. Feelings that were put away years ago had started to resurface and it felt like they were hanging off him everywhere for all to see. The more he tried to hide it the more it showed. He suddenly broke away from the stare, realising he had been holding his breath, letting out a sigh, he opened the gate for her.

"Thanks", she tugged on his beard playfully as she passed him. His mind was trying to be a friend, his heart, every day, wanting to be more.

The rest of the day went by pretty quickly. And the playful exchanges between Claire and Stuart had continued all day. By 6pm, the shearers had all finished for the day. Most of them were camping there overnight. Amy unloaded the food from the bags Michelle bought with her from the homestead and was getting dinner going. Davis cooked the bbq, because as far as he was concerned, no one burns chops like he can, he was tired but in good spirits. Claire again fed the lambs and settled them into a pen on the back verandah. Stuart lit the fire bucket, and the shearers were soon sitting around drinking cold beers and telling yarns.

Terry was telling everyone about some thefts that had been occurring at a neighbouring property, called Shallow River, where his girlfriend worked. Billy, Amy, and Claire were drinking their third bottle of wine, and the fits of teenage sounding giggles were growing louder by the glass, especially as Claire recounted the time that Billy tried to kiss her but lost his footing, falling into the bougainvillea bush. It was a story she loved to tell, it made him squirm, and she adored the blush it gave to his cheeks.

"I don't find it funny; I was serious you know", Billy divulged as they all looked at each other, then burst out laughing again. When the quiet came and most of the shearers had retired to their swags, Amy and Claire sat with their feet stretched out towards the fire bucket.

"I think there is definitely something going on between Dad and Michelle", Claire pondered.

"Wouldn't surprise me, they have been pretty close the last few years", Amy said, drinking the last of her wine. "Does it bother you?" Claire asked Amy seriously.

Amy sat up and faced Claire.

"I think, if he is happy, then I am", she replied, standing up with a slight stumble. "What about all the games you've been playing today?"

Claire looked at her sister with the utmost innocence.

"I see it, so does everyone else, you flirting your bum off with him".

"I was not,".

"Yeah, you were", Billy cut in.

"Think I might go to bed", Amy, a little bit pissed, pulled her pants up way too far, both Billy and Claire burst out laughing.

"Hate to say it, but I think I'm out as well," Billy laughed.

"Party pooooopers", Claire teased her. Amy knelt to wrap her arms about Claire's neck.

"Thanksyou for soming tome, i lub wu", she slurred as she wobbled off towards the house with Billy holding her up.

Claire sat for a while, tipping the wine bottle up high to get the last drop, when she heard a noise behind her. She turned sharply, with the bottle high in her hand ready to belt any strangers coming at her, and promptly slid off the chair onto the ground with a startled giggle. Stuart reached his hands out and pulled her up.

"What were you going to do with that?" He took the empty wine bottle out of her hand.

"I was going to clock the idiot sneaking up behind me", she said with a smug pout as he stared at her with an entertained expression. She tugged on his beard again, pointing out the strands of grey she could see. Looking up into his face, she laughed and took a deep breath before a small hiccup left her lips and she giggled again.

"I think I need to go to bed", she said, breaking the awkward moment.

Stuart smiled, wondering if she could even walk that far. He swept her up off her feet and into his arms in one movement. She looked, stunned, into his deep blue eyes, and for a moment, time seemed to go in slow motion as they looked at each other, she giggled and leant her head on his shoulder, and he rolled his eyes.

"Allow me to escort you to your room", he said in a smart arse manner as he held her closer to his chest. Claire tightened her grip about his neck as he pushed the main door open with her feet and he carried her upstairs.

Opening the bedroom door, he put her down, still grasping her hand tightly and led her over to her bed. It was near dark and completely silent. She sat on the edge of the bed, a soft glow from the hallway light breaking the darkness, he knelt beside her, sliding off her boots one at a time. Claire, despite a fair few wines, was still very present in the moment.

Stuart's touch was gentle and genuine. He knelt in front of her in the dimly lit room, resting his hands on her knees as he looked up into her eyes, reaching to wipe a tear from her cheek.

"You ok?" he asked softly. Stuart looked down and sighed deeply.

"I am sorry" she whispered.

"I have been angry for so many years, Claire, angry cause I didn't try harder, angry that I left you that weekend without really listening to you." He felt a lump growing in his throat.

Claire, with tears rolling down her face, leant down and pulled a wooden box from under the bed and opened it so he could see the pile of letters inside, the letters he had written to her 10 years ago when she first left. "I kept these".

Kneeling in front of her, he stared at his handwritten letters held neatly together by a red ribbon. Claire, untying the ribbon, shuffled through the pile and found one that was written in red pen and more wrinkled than the others.

"I've read this one the most, I want you to take it with you", she said handing it to him. He suddenly wanted to leave. He could feel himself nearly getting to a point he couldn't come back from.

"I better let you get some sleep", he stood quietly with the letter in his hand and pulled back the covers for her. She shuffled back, her head on the pillow looking up at him as he pulled the blankets up and tucked the sides in around her before he leant over gently and kissed her forehead, his beard tickling her cheek. Stuart smiled and turned to look at her once more.

"Goodnight, pretty girl". He turned, walked towards the door, looked back at her one last time and shut the door behind him.

Day two of shearing started smoothly. By one in the afternoon, between the farm hands and the hired shearers, the job was done.

Davis and Terry were cleaning up the last lot of wool into the press. Amy still looked pretty green but was determined to hold her own and not cop shit off everyone for being hungover.

Michelle cleaned up from lunch and loaded the boxes of remaining food and drinks onto the back of Stuart's ute, taking a seat along the fence with Davis and the shearers for one last beer. No one even noticed a car coming up the drive, until it came around the corner. The paddy wagon pulled up in front of the shearing shed.

Amy stood inside, watching out the small window closely, the door opened as two police officers got out and chatted to Michelle, Davis, and Terry. Amy grabbed Stuart by the shirt and pulled him over to the window nearly knocking him off his feet.

"Do you know who that is?" Looking out at the dark-haired copper with the Ray Ban sunglasses. Stuart studied him for a moment before it clicked.

"That's Eddie", he stated bluntly.

"If Claire sees him...." leaving the thought open, but it was too late. Claire had come around the side of the shed carrying the last of trays from lunch, stopped dead in her tracks, and dropped them with a horrendous crash.

"Claire", Eddie blurted out, surprised at seeing her for the first time in over 10 years. He moved towards her, trying to help pick up the mess. As he reached for her arm to help her up, she pushed him away. Claire stood up unable to move, her eyes fixed on her mother's killer. Stuart, already halfway down the shed stairs, watched her eyes furiously welling up with tears. He met her at the bottom of the steps, she grabbed his arm and looked up with her eyes full of tears.

"Get me out of here," she pleaded.

He took her hand with no emotion, no hesitation. Passing the tray to Amy who came down the stairs behind him, he nodded a respectful goodbye to Eddie, and led Claire by the hand past them and opened the door to his ute for her. He quickly walked to the other side, got in, started it up, tipped his hat goodbye to Davis who nodded approvingly back, and put his foot down hard, sending dust into the air as he drove away.

Chapter 6

Stuart pulled the ute into the opening between two thick lines of pine trees, got out and opened the gate across the track to Grinners, a small swimming hole a little way along Bailey's fire trail in the common that their property neighboured. Its proper name was Grinner Falls because the shape of the falls itself looks much like a smile.

The sun was getting low, creating patterns of gold along the water's edge, glistening between the long grasses. Stuart drove down the track that was nothing more than two dirt lines in the tall grass. The bush was thick along the creek side for a few kilometres or so before it opened into a flat grassy area where the rocky swimming hole sat at the base of a slight incline, the trees forming a natural canopy over the water. Stuart got out, walked around to her door, opened it, and reached his hand out.

"Let's go", he told her firmly, looking at her tear-stained cheeks. She took his hand without question; she knew he wasn't going to take no for an answer.

He unbuttoned his shirt and hung it on the bull bar as he put his toe to the back of his boots to slide them off.

"I don't have any togs", she stated in protest, her eyes shifting across his sculpted chest.

"Neither do I", his eyes locked to hers, sliding off his jeans, he was standing in front of her in just his boxers. He gave her a cheeky, sarcastic smile, then bolting across the grass, he launched himself off the largest boulder and into the water. Claire stood with a surprised look on her face. "If you don't hurry up, I'll come get you," Stuart said cheekily.

She sighed and rolled her eyes. Turning her back to him she slid off her boots and unbuttoned her jeans sliding them off and hanging them on the bull bar next to his. He drifted across the water, unable to take his eyes off her. She unzipped the little zipper at the top of her shirt and pulled it over her head. Claire was tanned. Her beautiful, naturally curly hair reached the top of her underwear in a point. With a deep breath she turned and walked out onto the same boulder Stuart had just jumped from. Her matching bra and underwear set was black, and the bra had a section of lace along the top of the cup. Her toned body gave him goose bumps. She tied her hair on top of her head in a cute loose bun and slid off the rock into the water.

The water was cool and refreshing and she could feel the stone covered bottom smoothly on the soles of her feet. Stuart smiled as he drifted towards her, his big muscular arms pushing the water to the sides. Little ripples that fanned off his floating beard made her laugh. They swam happily out to the falls, which pounded hard on her head as they passed through the sheet of water into the cave behind.

"I never knew there was a cave here" she yelled; the sound of the water pounding was intense. The sheet of white water was like moving crystal, loud and so beautiful.

He lifted himself up to sit on the dark ledge of rock and reached his hand down to pull her up beside him. The cave behind the waterfall was the size of a small car and had a tall rocky ceiling. She stood up, reaching her hands to lightly touch the rock above her.

Stuart stood up beside her with little droplets of water rolling off the end of his beard. She held her hand out to catch the drops and then pulled away shyly as her fingertips touched his chest. He moved towards her; despite the thunder-like noise of the falls she could hear his every breath. Taking her hand, he wrapped his big arms around her gently, unable to look into his eyes, she looked down, her hands pressed flat to his sculpted chest. He thought about what had just happened and looked into her eyes.

"Are you ok?", he mouthed silently.

His muscular arms around her felt strong and she forgot about Eddie. She nodded and watched him entwine his fingers amongst hers. Her stomach burned like fire as she looked up into his face, not able to shift her gaze from his deep blue eyes, they were gentle and comforting. She played with his beard and twisted it around her fingers. As though her body knew what her heart was aching for, it took over, her eyes closed as his forehead carefully touched hers. Without thinking, she lifted her head and gently kissed him. His lips were warm and soft. Her heart pounded so heavily she felt like it was going to come right out of her chest, her arms wrapped around his neck even tighter. He stopped, looked into her eyes, water dripping off his nose, and he rested his face down onto her shoulder. She could feel his breath on her neck and softly in her ear as he kissed her gently on the cheek. He cupped her cheeks in his hands, slowly moving his lips to kiss her again this time harder, more intense, moving his tongue around hers gently. It was soft but fierce with passion. He kissed the tip of her nose and rested his forehead again against hers and for that moment she couldn't move. It was like the world had stopped until she couldn't help but giggle at his beard tickling her top lip. Pulling from her embrace, red faced and with a smile, he stroked his beard back into place, he stood beside her feeling giddy, took her hand, rolling his eyes at her childish giggles.

"Ready", he yelled. She smiled a soft smile before he counted to three, they both took a few steps and jumped back through the wall of water into the open air, landing in the pool below.

Claire wasn't sure how long they had been behind the falls, but it was nearly dark when they reached the side of the same smooth rock they jumped in from. He lifted himself out of the water reaching down to take her hand to lift her out.

Stuart walked back to the ute and pulled a blanket from the tray and wrapped it around her.

"I don't want to go home", she insisted shortly. Raising an eyebrow, and for a moment lost in thought, he climbed up onto the tray, threw down a swag and a duffle bag full of his footy clothes.

"Let's stay here then," he concluded. Stuart wasted no time gathering a few river stones and arranged them into a circle lighting a small campfire in the middle before it became completely dark. He rolled out the swag next to the ute in front of the fire. Going through his footy duffle bag he pulled on a pair of trackies. Remembering that Michelle had left the box with the leftover food from lunch in the back of the ute, he pulled the box down and unpacked an impromptu picnic. "Jackpot!" he exclaimed with a smile.

Claire was sitting cross-legged in his team footy shirt with just her undies under on the swag. She unwrapped a salad sandwich.

"I've never seen a footy shirt look so damn sexy", he shared, admiring her in his clothes. She smiled and her cheeks turned a rosy pink. "I'll let you wear it on my next game, you can be my good luck charm".

"Thank you for this," Claire said, taking a bite of the sandwich.

"I am all for coming to the rescue of a damsel in distress", he said with a smile, unwrapping the cooked chicken legs and potato salad from the box. With plastic cups, knives, and forks, they had quite the gourmet feast. He took the half bottle of Jack Daniels from behind the driver's seat and filled two of the plastic cups, passing one to her.

"I mean it, Stuart". Claire was serious. Stuart stood facing her in front of the fire in just the pair of trackies, his thick chest looked like warm bronze in the fire light, she could see the glow of dirty blonde hairs scattered across his chest.

"I just don't want to go back home tonight", she said looking down at her sandwich.

"He would have gone by now, I know you blame him, I know he hurt you, but being the local copper, you are going to have to talk to him sooner or later, Claire", Stuart sighed.

"I just can't stand the sight of him", she rubbed her face.

Stuart reached into his footy bag and pulled out an envelope, it was the letter written in red pen she had given him. Something had changed between them that afternoon, she could feel it. Kneeling beside her, he grabbed her hand, she watched him play with her fingertips.

"You know, I don't know how many times I have read this since you gave it to me". He held the envelope carefully, she softly tugged at his long beard. "I still mean every word that is written here", he said as he gave it back to her.

"I've felt so lost since coming home, with Dad, also with you, it was Bill who convinced me to not give up", Claire whispered, fighting tears away.

Stuart, with down cast eyes, sighed, he took her hand and played with her fingers again as she lay down and put her head on the swag's pillow.

"I'm glad you kept my letters", he smiled.

With silence in the air by the crackling fire she felt him slide into the swag behind her, wrapping his strong arms around her and pulling her close to his chest, his beard tickling her neck. He fought his heart with everything he had not to go too far. He rested his head on the pillow behind hers, her hair smelled like strawberries. He wanted to tell her how much he loved having her in his arms, he was guarded, however, she still had not decided to stay and he didn't want to get hurt again, it almost physically hurt to keep her at arm's length. Before long she was asleep. He held her for most of the night. As she sleepily rolled over to face him, he held her even tighter, opening his eyes, he watched her sleep until the glow of the last of the coals was gone. He breathed her in, gently kissed her nose, and closed his eyes.

Chapter 7

Claire sat patiently waiting for her father as he finished his 3rd chemo treatment. He was now completely bald, and he looked even more frail than usual. Dr Wong called her into his office.

"Miss Gannon, my name is Yen Wong", he held out his hand for a weak handshake. "Your father has listed you as his emergency contact and his next of kin for his treatment".

"Yes, that's correct".

"Wonderful, your father will have one more session of chemo in a few weeks' time, which will be his 4th and last of the course, I would like to reassess him then.".

"What other treatment will he receive?" she asked.

"For now, just the chemo, we will do a full PET scan a week after his 4th session to determine if it has been effective".

Claire sighed. "When you originally diagnosed him, you said he might have up to 18 months, that was five months ago", she said.

"Yes, and for now that will remain the same until we can see if the chemo has been successful at shrinking the tumour." Dr Wong said.

"What about surgery to remove the tumour?" she asked in frustration.

"I will make that decision after the scans, until then, keep up with the aftercare and I'll see you on the next visit", he said, rising from his chair and ushering her out, quickly closing the door to his office behind her.

"Well, that was a waste of bloody time", she mumbled to herself as she saw Dad waiting for her.

Again, the drive home was a quiet one. Claire was left to think about her own life and what had happened between her and Stuart. She knew he was holding back until she made up her mind about staying. She couldn't get him out of her mind, the feeling of his arms around her by the fire. Also, the idea of teaching still lingered in her mind.

Dad was helped upstairs and into bed by Terry and Michelle.

She hoped it would get easier, seeing him so weak, but it never did, she felt low and drained. Stuart knocked on her bedroom door later that afternoon.

"Want to come for a drive?"

She looked intrigued and pulled her boots on and a cardigan.

"Where are we going?" she asked him as he opened the passenger door for her.

"It's a surprise". Stuart loved to keep her guessing, driving them down the back road towards the river. It was late afternoon; he pulled the ute onto the main road heading for Reffshore. Claire was more and more curious as to where they were going.

"How are you holding up?"

"I'd be so much better if you would tell me where we are going".

Stuart pulled into the carpark of the CWA ladies hall and opened the door for her. The carpark was packed.

"I thought you could use some time out", Stuart said, fishing deep into his pocket for a pair of tickets. "The ladies are having a movie here tonight, *Out of Africa*, I know it's corny but if I had told you, would you have come?" He grabbed a blanket from the back of the ute. She wrinkled her nose as he took her hand and led the way into the paddock behind the hall where a large screen had been erected for an open-air movie night.

"Is this a date?" she asked smiling.

"Maybe". He said quietly.

Claire's heart felt full. Her body had goosebumps from head to toe as he lay the blanket against one of the sets of hay bales dotted around the grass. A nearby table was filled with buckets of popcorn and a variety of chocolates. She took her place on the blanket next to him as he lay out three buckets of popcorn and popped the cork out of the bottle of wine he had bought.

In the darkness she could see at least one hundred people watching the movie. She had no idea he had planned this, and as he filled her glass of wine, she sat cross legged and completely engrossed in Meryl Streep, as secretly, it was one of her favourite movies.

He smiled, watching her smile, after a while she leaned into him with her head resting lightly on his shoulder.

He leant his head on hers and wrapped the blankets tighter around them. It was a magical night. She really felt a spark between them the last few weeks and the fact that he had gone to so much trouble to arrange this surprise impressed her. It was nearly 1am when Stuart pulled into *November,* taking her home.

"Thank you for a wonderful night, I really, really loved it", Claire said, smiling uncontrollably.

"I had a good time too, thank you for coming", Stuart blushed as he walked around and opened her door for her.

Claire smiled as he walked her onto the verandah. She felt awkward, her stomach full of butterflies, as he said goodnight, gently kissing her on the cheek. She couldn't remember the last time she felt this happy.

A few days later, Stuart was loading his ute with a heavy suitcase, as Claire walked down the driveway towards Grove Cottage to see him. He had been distant since their date, and she felt as though he was avoiding her.

"Are you going somewhere?" she asked, watching as he lifted a second suitcase into his ute.

"I'm going to Melbourne, my brother was in an accident last night and the doctors have called for the family", he said sadly.

"Oh, Stuart, I'm so sorry", she murmured, reaching out to touch his arm. He shied away from her, walking around the other side of the ute to secure the bags. "Is there anything I can do?" she asked, feeling helpless.

"No", he said shortly. He shut the door to the cottage and closed the picket fence gate after him.

"I have to go", he admitted softly with a weak smile and opened the door of the ute before stopping himself to look at her. He had been avoiding being alone with her since their date. He felt he had to keep his distance until he knew for sure if she was planning to stay, he could feel himself falling in love with her all over again, deeper than he ever had before. He walked back to Claire.

"Look after yourself and your dad, ok", he said, as he kissed her on the cheek, breathing in her perfume. She tried to put her arms around him, but he stopped her. Holding her hands and looking into her now teary eyes, he smiled softly and touched the side of her face with his hand.

"I'm sorry, Claire, I have to go", he said again. This time he didn't stop, nor did he look back as he drove down the main driveway headed for the road.

She found herself standing in the middle of the gravel road watching him drive away, she didn't know how long she had been standing there before she just sat down.

Stuart turned onto the highway feeling terrible. It was so painful for him to keep her at arm's length, in fact he had almost turned around several times since driving away. He had been wrestling with his heart ever since the movies, he could see and feel her anguish every time he looked at her. He could see her not understanding why he had to wait before getting into a relationship again. He needed to know he wasn't jumping in headfirst if she wasn't going to be there to catch him.

Billy and Amy stood in the yards watching Claire sitting on the driveway. Eventually she stood up and walked back toward the homestead, kicking rocks along the way. She suddenly started running, faster and faster, past them both and upstairs, into her room, shutting the door. She slumped down on the floor against her bed with her head in her knees and let out a sorrowful moan as she released the built-up emotion deep inside her and cried uncontrollably.

She didn't fully understand, the time at the falls was amazing, the date they had at the open-air movies was amazing, what was wrong with Stuart? She thought about that night, replaying being behind the waterfall with him, his kiss, his strong arms. It's all she could think about. His strong body against hers as she kissed him... "Stop it, Claire", she snapped at herself.

Dad came down for dinner that evening. Despite the shine he now had on his head from lack of hair he was in good spirits. Claire picked at her chicken. She wasn't hungry. She felt lonely and decided to go to bed early. A quiet knock came on her bedroom door as she sat in bed typing an email to Pia on her laptop. Michelle came in with a tray.

"I bought you some apple pie," she smiled, placing the bowl down on the bed beside her.

"Thanks", she mumbled in a sombre voice, picking up the bowl. Looking at the slice of pie, with a generous scoop of ice-cream beside it, she dug her spoon in, and jammed it into her mouth, emotional eating at its finest.

"What's wrong?" Michelle asked, finally looking to her for answers.

Claire sighed. "Promise you won't tell anyone".

Michelle nodded. "Of course."

Claire spooned another giant piece of pie into her mouth, talking with her mouth full. "It's probably nothing, maybe I am reading too much into it", Claire whined.

Michelle looked at her, puzzled, trying to make out the pie crust language she was mumbling.

"Stuart and I kissed", Claire said, scooping another piece into her mouth. "It was wonderful, I think we had some kind of moment the other night, then he took me on the most amazing date in town at the movies, but he has been really weird since, even avoiding me now", she sighed, swallowing the last of the mouthful.

"Do you want to hear the truth, Claire?" Michelle asked seriously.

Claire nodded taking another big mouthful of pie. "I'm not sure who was more devastated the day you left, Stuart or your father".

Claire looked up at her again, swallowing hard.

"I knew for months that he had feelings for you, I actually found out by accident", she softly placed her hand on Claire's knee in a sign of comfort.

"He told me before I left that he had feelings for me", Claire said, swirling her spoon in the bowl.

"More than *feelings* sweetie, that boy is in love with you, I'm sure of that". Michelle tilted her head with a soft smile.

Claire looked down at her plate.

"He has barely spoken to me in days though, and now he has gone, for who knows how long. I just feel lost", she said sadly taking the last of the apple pie on her spoon.

Michelle smiled, taking the empty bowl.

"Give him time, I bet he feels just as lost as you do; besides you have your life to sort out also". Michelle said standing. "What is it that you want?".

"I didn't know I wanted anything when I got back, I was just coming for a few days to see Dad," she groaned, having another ugly cry.

"Follow your heart". Michelle squeezed Claire's hand before heading back downstairs.

Claire lay quietly watching the candle flame flicker mosaic patterns on the ceiling. Finally, she stood up, put on her robe and slippers, walked down the hall to her father's room, and knocked quietly.

"Come in". She pushed the door open.

"Hey Daddy", she said, making herself comfortable in his lazy boy recliner beside the bed.

"I'm fine," he said suddenly.

Claire looked at Dad and laughed. She really had missed him.

"Hey Dad", she said softly with a small lump building in her throat.

"Would you mind if I moved back home?" she asked after a brief silence.

Davis looked up at her with a big smile. "Of course, I don't mind", he said, holding a hand over his heart with pride. "What are you going to do about your place in Perth?"

"The lease is up for renewal; I have a friend living there at the moment, and I know she would be happy to take over. It was fully furnished when I moved in so it wouldn't take much to pack up", she babbled on, a million things running through her mind at once. Dad happily listened to her ramblings. He had missed it.

"Just means I'll have to leave you and go back to Perth for a few days to get my things and sign off on some details with the real estate, probably should formally quit my job too, I guess", she said with a laugh. "The boss is a piece of work anyway".

"I'm not going to go anywhere, I'll still be kicking when you get back", he laughed.

Davis sat forward on his pillows, deep in thought. "I don't want you to go alone, why don't you take your sister with you", he suggested. Claire pondered on the idea.

"Thanks Dad", she leaned in for a hug.

Claire lay in bed unable to sleep. She felt relieved that she had decided to come home. She didn't want to lose any more time with her father, she had lost 10 years with him and couldn't bear the thought of him dying and her not being there.

She picked up her phone once again and still no messages.

She opened the message folder and selected Stuart's name to open a new text message.

"Hi, it's Claire, I just wanted to say that I hope you are ok", she wrote, then deleted it, then wrote it again and then procrastinated for half an hour about sending it. "I am heading back to Perth for a few days, I hope you are ok" she studied the message for 10 minutes then hit the send and it was done, "Can't take it back now", she thought.

Chapter 8

The sun was hot that morning as she drove her little blue car into Reffshore. Not a cloud in the sky, it was going to be a sweltering day. Bringing back all sorts of crazy memories of teenage stupidity, she pulled into the carpark at Reffshore Central High School. After a quick chat with an older man in the office, she stood in the foyer of her old school waiting for Lisa.

The door to the principal's office opened and Lisa came out to meet her with a warm hug.

"Graeme said you were back in town," she led Claire into the office holding her hand out to a nearby chair.

"Thanks for seeing me, Lisa, I really appreciate it, I know you're busy", Claire started, then slid across a bundle of stapled papers.

"I wanted to give you my resume, if by chance there were any teaching positions coming up next term", she stammered nervously.

Lisa looked delighted going through her resume.

"You have not taught a class for a few years?" she said, taking a sip of her coffee.

"No, I have, just not full time, but I am keen to get back into it, I lost quite a lot of motivation when I left, only doing casual teaching", she looked down.

"I have decided to move back home so I thought I should start to think about the future, it was always something I wanted to do", she said more confidently.

Lisa looked through a small folder, then sifted through the crinkled pages of the address index on the desk.

"If you want to start slow next term, I can put you down for a casual relief position, when you are ready to go full time, we can talk again", she said with a smile.

Claire sat back in the chair pondering the thought.

"I'd love to do some casual classes; my dad is dying so I'd like to not commit myself to full time yet".

"No worries at all, I'll put you on the call list for next term", Lisa said, handing her a small card for her to write her details on.

"Mrs Anderson is going on maternity leave at the end of the year and Mr Grant is set to try and retire for the third time, so there will be a lot of options coming up", Lisa said, putting Claire's card into the index box.

"Thank you, Lisa, I really owe you one", Claire replied eagerly.

"It's really my pleasure, come for a walk if you have time, I'll show you around, it's been quite some time since you were here," she said with a cheeky grin.

Lisa walked her down the corridor, past several offices and out another door into the undercover area at the back. The school was classed as a small school and all the classroom buildings were the same as when she went to school, all opening onto the central undercover area. A football oval was at the back as well as the agriculture buildings alongside various yards and fenced gardens.

On the left side of the office was the hall which had a basketball court inside, it also had a stage area that was used as part of the drama classes. Most of the science classrooms were new since she had been there, a kitchen and hospitality area were also new, leading down through another undercover walkway to the bus bays.

Lisa and Claire chatted about the mischief they got up to in high school. Walking back through the office, Lisa gave her another hug.

"Thank you again, Lisa, I'm really excited to get back into teaching", she said goodbye and walked back to her car. Claire pulled out her phone and texted Stuart. "I got a job, feeling excited to be putting life back together slowly, I hope you're ok, Claire."

Driving back through town, she pulled into the supermarket and grabbed a trolley. The quick trip to pick up a few items turned into a trolley load. As she neared the deli section, she looked over to the woman serving, taking a deep breath in, she clenched her fists. The woman serving looked up at her and smiled, it was Emma, Eddies wife.

"Can I help you?" she said in a careful voice.

"I'll just grab a kilo of bacon, please", Claire said politely. Emma wrapped the bacon and passed it over the top of the servery to Claire.

"Is there anything else I can get for you?" Emma asked.

Claire remembered what Stuart had said to her about having to see Eddie sooner or later, and even though he wasn't here, seeing Emma brought those same feelings to the fore and she just didn't have the energy to analyse it right now. Claire took a breath and made sure she was as nice as she could possibly be, as much as she wanted to peg the wrapped bacon as hard as she could back over the servery.

"No, thank you", she said quickly, and pushed her trolley into the produce section. After a quick trip through the checkout, she packed her groceries into the car and took the trolley back to the bay at the front of the supermarket. All she wanted to do was go home.

"Claire?", she heard a voice call. She turned to see Emma walking towards her. She could feel the hairs on her neck standing on end at the sight of her coming. She stood there, staring blankly, as Emma came closer.

"I wondered if you had some time for a chat?" she asked in a hopeful voice.

Claire looked around, trying to think of a reason to say no, but couldn't find one.

"We could have a coffee if you have some time now, my shout", Emma asked her.

Claire sighed and pressed the button on the remote for the car and locked the doors.

"Sure, why not", Claire muttered shortly. Emma smiled and led her quietly to Maxie's café, not too far down the main street. Emma ordered them both coffee.

They sat at a window table, awkwardly waiting for the waitress to bring the coffee over.

"I know you probably don't want to talk to me, and I understand that, Eddie said he saw you the other day and that you took off", Emma started carefully.

Claire gave a rough smile raising an eyebrow as she stirred her recently delivered coffee.

"Eddie is so sorry about what happened to Karen, it is something he still has nightmares about, he was so devastated at your reaction seeing him the other week". Emma was trying hard to defend her husband.

"I am sorry, Claire, I'm sorry it turned out the way it did, it was over 10 years ago now, I guess I am hoping you can forgive him and perhaps, one day, we can all be friends again", Emma looked seriously at Claire. "Eddie and I have been married for eight years now and I know he would love to heal from the accident as much as you, it wasn't his fault."

If it was physically possible to have steam coming out your ears, Claire was sure she would at that moment.

"You're right, it was years ago, and I know you think he didn't mean to hurt me, but he did, he killed my mother, forgiveness is not something I can think about right now". Drinking the last of her coffee, Claire stood and put her bag on her shoulder pushing her chair in carefully. "Oh, as for being friends, you can guess my answer to that question."

Emma looked down at her cup sadly.

"Thanks for the coffee, but I need to go", Claire left quickly without looking back nor giving a second thought.

Chapter 9

Claire and Amy flew out of Reffshore Regional Airport early the next Wednesday to Adelaide, then onto another flight to Perth.

Amy was excited and could hardly sit still the whole way.

Claire had an organised list of what she needed to do and where she needed to go.

First, she and Amy would check into their motel, it seemed a better idea for them to stay there rather than pile into the little apartment that was really not hers anymore. She would need to pack her belongings into boxes and arrange delivery back home, then onto the real estate where she needed to sign her apartment over to Pia, and lastly call in to Hobb's Bar and Grill and hand in her resignation, amongst other things. With so much to do she thought she would go mad. She had not heard from Stuart, despite leaving him a few more messages, and that played on her mind also.

She let out an enormous sigh as the flight attendant pushed the cart down the aisle collecting the empty cups and rubbish ready to land.

Amy was keen to get back to Perth, she had made some good friends there during her visits and she was planning a catch up that night. Claire was 30. There was a significant age gap between her and Amy, and Amy had spent quite a few of her school holidays in Perth growing up at her place.

The plane came in smoothly. Claire felt the heat hit her like a brick wall as they walked out of the terminal. Strangely enough, she didn't feel anything when she got there except her urgent need to get back to her father.

Claire hired a car at the airport. They had decided that it was too far to drive her car back to Perth; it had taken her 3 days driving just to get to Victoria in the first place.

The trip to the motel was easy for her, she knew her way around. Their apartment was spacious and had 2 bedrooms on each side of a large lounge room and kitchen that opened onto a large balcony looking over the ocean. She had missed the salt air and breathed it in deep as she stood looking out over the beach dotted with cafes and alfresco dining areas. It was busy, but she found it comforting in some ways.

Amy was quick to unpack, pulling out an outfit to go out in.

"I need to tell you something. I met someone, and I think I really like him".

Claire smiled with her hands on her hips. "And who is this mystery guy?".

"I met him at the hospital last time I was there with ad, he is a doctor".

Claire rolled her eyes. "What time are your friends picking you up?" she said, watching her flat ironing her blonde hair.

"At 5, so that leaves me 2 hours to get ready". Claire laughed and rolled her eyes again before picking her bag up, saying a quick goodbye to Amy and heading out the door.

Pia greeted Claire with a mammoth hug. "It's so good to see you".

"The place looks great", Claire said as she looked around at the new shabby chic decor. Mismatched knickknacks dotted the shelves, and there was a round sofa and cane egg chair. A large silver wine rack stood near the island bench in the kitchen with a large wide leaf plant on top. Pia poured them a glass of wine each and they sat at the little white table and chairs in the courtyard.

"I packed all your bits and pieces for you a month ago, they are downstairs in the garage ready to go", she said sadly.

"A month ago?" Claire gasped in shock.

"I just knew, deep down, you would not come back even though I never thought I'd see the day", Pia said taking a sip of wine and smiling fondly at her friend.

"Me too, but it's funny, it feels right, my dad needs me home and, truthfully, I think I'm ready to go back, think I might try for a teaching job too", Claire said.

"Wow, life has changed for you, I'm so glad you have found your way", Pia said, holding her glass up to toast her friend as their glasses clinked together, then taking a big mouthful.

"You look happier and refreshed. Hang on a minute......who is he?" Pia noticed suddenly.

Claire blushed a dark shade of red.

"Oh my god, there is a Mr", Pia wiggled in her chair with delight watching her friend cringe with the pressure of answering.

"It's Stuart actually. I kissed him, in a cave, behind a waterfall", Claire remembered with a smile.

"What!! Sounds like something from a movie. This, Stuart, is the letter writing guy, yes?" Pia asked, trying to place Stuart.

"Yeah, that's the one", Claire smiled.

"Awwww, that is so romantic. Who kisses people in waterfall caves?" She asked, falling dramatically back on the chair with a sigh.

Claire laughed at her friend's antics as she took the last mouthful of wine.

"Let's go out for dinner, you can quit your job while we are at it, I can't wait to see the look on that cranky old duck's face when you tell her to fuck off", Pia laughed.

"I didn't bring anything to wear, I had not planned to go out, I thought I'd leave that up to my sister," Claire grumbled.

"Pfft, come into my world", Pia said as she waved her hands in front of her face magically as she led her into the walk-in robe to find the perfect ensemble.

Claire and Pia walked into Hobb's Bar and Grill at around 7pm. Claire walked back into the kitchen area to find Mrs Harris; her not-so-nice boss wasn't there.

"Hey, you're back", a voice came. It was Frank. Frank was the chef, a fine cook indeed and he knew it. He was short and podgy with a chef's hat hiding his balding, up-himself head.

"Nah, I am here to resign," Claire said, shaking Frank's hand.

"She isn't here, lucky you," Frank braced himself slicing into an obscenely large onion.

"Ahhh, well, you will have to give it to her for me, Frankie", Claire begged with a cheeky grin. Frank looked at her with a blank, unimpressed face.

"Pin it on the board and I'll deal with her, even though she wrote you out of the rosters months ago", he grunted.

Claire wrapped her arms about his thick shoulders and squeezed as hard as she could, planting a kiss on his cheek.

"I owe you one, Frankie, thank you", she said.

He blushed as she gave him another hug, raised his chubby, stuck-up hand and waved her out of his kitchen.

"Go on, get out and take all that soppy shit with you".

Claire wore faux leather pants and a loose-fitting white blouse, her hair was in a neat ponytail, a black and gold bag with matching high heels finishing the outfit. Pia had expensive taste in clothes, and she couldn't help feeling like a million bucks. Pia was in a floral top, short black skirt and wedge heels that showed her long, tanned legs off perfectly. They sat on the boardwalk and ate a spectacular seafood dinner.

"Ahh, this is what I will miss about Perth", Claire said, pouring herself another glass of red wine.

"I couldn't give it up", Pia mused as she looked out over the crashing waves on one side and the lights of the city high and bright on the other.

They sat at the bar in one of the waterfront clubs and chatted about life, it was nearly 10.30pm when Pia joined up with a few of her friends and headed off to another club. Pia gave her friend a hug,

"Are you sure you won't come, will you be right?" she asked waving to her friends who were waiting for her.

"Yeah, my motel isn't far, I might walk and soak up the city lights", she released Pia from their embrace.

"I'll catch up with you at the real estate tomorrow", she said as Pia joined her friends.

Claire took off her heels and walked down to the water's edge feeling the sand between her toes, the lights from the city behind reflected dots of gold in the water. She checked her phone to find several missed calls, a number she didn't recognise. She swiped the screen and dialled back the number in case it was an emergency.

"Hello", a woman's voice answered.

"Hi, my name is Claire Gannon, I had quite a few missed a few calls from this number," she said nervously.

"Oh yes, one moment", the woman said. There was a delayed silence. The phone picked up again "Hello...Claire?". She instantly recognised the comforting voice.

"Hey there", she said to Stuart with her heart bulging in her throat, instantly wanting to cry. "I'm sorry if I disturbed you earlier", he said shortly.

"You didn't, I'm sorry I missed your calls, I was having dinner with Pia and the music was so loud I just didn't hear it", she apologised quickly, her mind was telling her to say so many things and she felt like she was going in seven directions at once.

"I'm back here in Perth", she said softly sitting down on the sand.

"Yeah, Michelle told me, I am sorry I didn't get back in time to say goodbye", he said. She could hear the sadness in his voice. Claire thought on his words for a moment and came to the conclusion that he didn't get her texts.

"Did you not get my messages?" she asked with her heart pounding hard.

"What messages?" he asked shortly. She sighed heavily and could feel the lump coming hard in her throat and her eyes welled up at the thought of him thinking she had left again.

"I texted your number the night after you left and several times since", she left it hanging.

"I have not had a mobile for years, Claire, I am using my sister-in-law's at the moment, that's who answered. What messages did you leave?" he asked, leaving a silence on the phone that could have shattered glass.

This was the moment she had been waiting for, to tell him she was moving home, what if he didn't feel anything for her anymore after all? She was about to walk right out on the ledge.

"I was seeing if you were ok, told you I had a job and letting you know that I was going back to Perth to sort out my apartment, cause I made the decision to move back home", she said with a shaky voice as she fought hard to keep her tears at bay. She was nervous, her stomach was in knots.

"Oh", was all he said. The awkward silence that followed on the phone could have slapped her in the face. She hung on the silence.

"Are you still there?" she said softly as she started to cry. What had she done? Her worst fears had just leapt up from the sand right in front of her. Was she right about him not being happy to hear the news?

As the silence lingered on the phone, she put her head down and cried hard.

"Stuart?" she sobbed.

"Yeah, I'm here," barely a whisper.

That's it, she had blown it, she felt like she was being stabbed with a hundred knives. She wiped her face and sat listening to the silence.

"Please talk to me", she whispered.

"My brother died on Tuesday, his funeral is Friday, I rang cause there was no one else's voice in the world I wanted to hear but yours", he whispered. He was sobbing quietly, Claire cried harder listening to him, her heart ached hearing his pain.

"I'm so sorry, Stuart", she said softly into the phone as she wiped the tears away.

"I wasn't sure if you wanted to talk to me, you didn't say much when you left, I'm sorry I should have rung you sooner, but that would not have mattered since you don't have a phone anyway and here I am leaving messages for god knows who to read...," she rambled nervously.

"You have no idea, do you?", Stuart said calmly. She stopped and listened.

"I'm ......", he was gone, followed by a beep as her phone ran out of battery and turned itself off.

"What...no...nooo ...you fucking stupid, bloody, phone!" she cursed taking off at a full blown run, phone in one hand, shoes in the other, down the beach towards her motel. She stood impatiently in the elevator with her feet covered in sand till it clicked over finally to the 14th floor, she desperately ran down the hallway and fell through her apartment door as the key card glowed green to open. Pulling all the clothes out of her suitcase, throwing them into the air to find her phone charger she plugged it in, it wasn't working "fuck!" she yelled in frustration. Finally, her phone had just enough battery to turn on. She dialled back the number, tapping her hand on the table with the jitters. An automated message said:

"The phone you are calling is switched off or unavailable". Claire slumped down the wall and sat on the floor staring at her phone for 20 minutes before trying again with the same response.

Claire undressed and put on her pyjama pants with a white singlet top. She lay in bed watching her phone on charge beside her for any signs of life. She didn't want to send the number a text in case it wasn't Stuart who was reading it. Maybe she should go to Melbourne and go to his brother's funeral. What would he say if she just turned up there? She played the conversation over and over in her head. Checking her phone once again it said it was 2.05am. Pulling the doona up around her face, still staring at her phone, she slowly drifted off to sleep.

Claire woke rather late the next morning and checked her phone to see no messages. 8.27am. She dragged herself out of bed with a yawn and into the lounge area to find Amy on the couch asleep, holding a foam cup of microwave noodles, the fork still in her hand with cold stiff noodles stuck to the prongs. She must have fallen asleep mid mouthful. With a giggle, she took the cup and put it on the table beside her drunken sister. It was

Thursday, one job left to do before heading home and that was signing her lease over to Pia.

Claire turned on the jug to make a coffee. Amy suddenly sat upright; she had startled herself awake. She was wearing the same clothes but with only one shoe and her hair looked like a giant ball of frizz.

"Good morning", Claire giggled. "Big night?"

Amy took off the single wedge, crawled along the carpet and slithered on to the bar stool in front of Claire.

"A great, big night, you wouldn't believe it, I hardly drank at all", she said with amazement.

"It's Dad's Birthday at the end of the month, I think we should do something," Claire said, placing a mug of strong coffee down in front of her sister.

"We could have a party, or have dinner in town at the pub", Amy leant back trying to think of ideas.

"Dad probably wouldn't want a ton of people at home, maybe we could do the dinner, the Royal Hotel has nice food and enough room to host a large group", Claire said.

"That's it then, let's organise it, keep it a secret cause he won't like the idea and will not come otherwise", Amy said.

"When we go to the real estate, there is a party supplies place not far away, we can call in and grab some stuff before we go home tomorrow", Claire said shortly, then, checking her phone again, let out a sigh.

"Expecting a call?" Amy asked, wiggling her eyebrows up and down.

"I spoke to Stuart last night, but the phone cut out mid conversation", she sighed.

Amy knew of her sister's letter writing affair, of sorts, with Stuart, but hadn't realised they were still an item.

"How long has this been going on?" Amy asked, very unimpressed with her sister keeping secrets.

"I'm not sure it is going on yet, although I kissed him, and he kissed me", Claire said with a smile.

"Where and when was this?" Amy asked with a cranky tone.

"The day Eddie turned up at the shearing shed, when we were at Grinner's in the cave behind the waterfall", she said looking starry eyed.

Amy laughed. "Sounds like something out of a movie". Thinking again about what Claire had said. "I didn't know there was a cave behind the falls".

"I spoke to him last night, he said his brother's funeral is Friday", Claire said "I think I should go", she was deep in thought.

Amy looked sternly at her sister. "What were you planning to do? Just turn up at the funeral, hi how you going? I am uninvited but I thought I'd come anyway", she said awkwardly. "What if he doesn't want you there?"

"It will just be a risk I'll have to take", Claire ended the conversation, walking towards her room.

"You can go to the party shop and fly home," Claire told her, again, checking her phone.

"Do you really think this is the right thing to do?" Amy asked again seriously.

"I don't know what the right thing to do is, Amy, I've not done the right thing for years," Claire stopped in the doorway to her room, "But I know I need to go and be there for him, I just feel it". Claire said, tapping her hand on her heart.

"Ok, but you need to come with me to the party shop before you go, cause I am hopeless at this kinda thing", Amy insisted looking suddenly like she was going to spew.

"Seriously?" Claire yelled, as Amy took off towards the bathroom. "Hardly drank a thing hey", Claire mumbled to herself.

A few hours later, Claire had signed the paperwork at the real estate office with Pia. As they were leaving, Pia handed Claire a bag with another outfit in it, this time a black outfit for the funeral, Claire wrapped her arms around her friend.

"Thank you for everything, I'll have these dry cleaned and sent back as soon as I get home".

"You keep them", Pia hugged her again. "Be safe."

"I hope I am doing the right thing", Claire said nervously.

"Only you can know what is right, if it feels right in your gut, go with that", Pia said. They then said their goodbyes.

Claire hugged her sister. Touching her chest and then pointed to Amy.

Claire phoned ahead to Michelle, letting her know Amy's flight would be boarding soon and so far, it was running on time. Billy would pick her up at the airport.

"I need the funeral info for Stuart's brother, I'm about to get on a flight to Melbourne". Claire's tone was serious.

"That is very considerate of you, Claire, but do you really think it's a good idea?" Michelle asked her.

"Probably not, I can hardly explain why, I just need to go", she whispered, trying to fight the tears away.

"I'll email you all the information Stuart gave your father but promise me you will be careful", she said, before wishing her luck and saying goodbye.

Chapter 10

Claire sat in the terminal waiting for her plane to board at 5pm. It was now 3.57, she would get into Melbourne at 9pm. She didn't have a plan and was just running on a whim, hoping it would be ok. The feeling of urgency was turning into some serious anxiety churning in her stomach.

Reading over her emails, she noted that a public service would be held at 11am at the North Chapel in Ashfield Memorial Gardens in the northeast suburb of Diamond Creek, followed by a graveside service for close family only. She checked her phone again. Still nothing. After a quick accommodation search, she found a room at the Oakland apartments and booked in, just as the flight was called to board.

Claire slept most of the way. The Jetstar flight was on time, and she landed in Melbourne not long after 9pm. She had not been to Melbourne since a school camp many years ago. The taxi ride from the airport gave her a chance to admire the beautiful city lights. She got the key from the reception desk and headed up to her room. The view of the city from the window was beautiful. She checked her phone, no messages except from Michelle, checking in to see how she was. She dialled home, feeling the need for the comfort of her father's advice. On the phone, he let her know that Amy had been safely picked up and was home, Davis calmly listened to his daughter, and she explained to him what her plans were.

"I'll be home in a few days, if not sooner, it's just something I need to do, Daddy", she said. Davis told her how much he loved her before saying goodnight. Laying in bed that night, it didn't take her long to fall asleep.

The sun glared brightly through the windows the next morning. After a shower, she did her makeup, braided her long hair, rolling it into a neat bun at the base of her head. The dress Pia had given her was black, had a high lace neck and short lace sleeves. It was tight across the top and flared out slightly to the knee, probably a bit too formal for a funeral but it was all she had. She put on a pair of low black heels that Pia had included in the bag. She looked quite sophisticated but felt so nervous she thought she would vomit.

The Memorial Gardens were beautiful. There were 3 small chapels amongst the gardens and hundreds of headstones scattered the lawn surrounding. It was a peaceful place. Following the signs, she found herself on the paved path near the North Chapel. There were at least a hundred people slowly filing in, signing the guestbook as they entered. Joining the end of the line, she signed her name and found her seat towards the back of the congregation. The auditorium was full of ornate floral arrangements and had several rows of chairs, and at the very front, a small stage area where the lectern sat. As the room quickly filled, she realised she didn't know anyone, she felt like an intruder, like a stranger more than ever.

After a few moments, the young lady playing the piano at the side of the room signalled the start of the service. Another musician then played a slow piece on the violin, everyone was instructed to stand as six men carried a dark-stained wooden coffin down the aisle, placing it on the stand at the front of the room. She could see Stuart; he was one of the pall bearers. All six men wore black suits and light blue ties as a tribute to his brother's many years served in the ambulance services, according to the program.

Stuart sat next to his mum as the service started. The funeral director, according to the program Claire received when she entered the chapel, took her place behind the lectern, starting the service.

The first hymn was Amazing Grace, and everyone stood while singing the song. As Stuart was introduced to read his brother's eulogy and took his place at the lectern, she suddenly wished she had not come. He spoke confidently to the crowd, looking up, he scanned the faces, looking down and checking his notes and again addressing the mourners before, finally, she caught his eye. He stopped speaking briefly, looking at her, he slowly smiled then introduced a slideshow of photo memories to celebrate his brother's life, before taking his seat again next to his mother.

After 2 more hymns and a reading, the lady invited the mourners to come and lay any floral tributes at the front. Stuart turned in his seat, again trying to find her in the faces of people behind him but couldn't see her. The lady at the lectern advised the people that the burial would now take place and was to be attended by those invited only and the rest of the guests should accompany her to the gazebo area to the side of the main doors for light refreshments.

When the music started, the doors at the back opened and eight uniformed Ambulance officers walked down the aisle and stood on either side of the door in salute as the six men who carried in the coffin carried it back out to the waiting hearse. The rows of people filed back through the doors one by one, and Claire waited till the last row left before joining the line to leave. She watched people comforting each other, some smiling, some crying, some laughing.

Stuart searched the mourners for her, and after a while, he saw her standing quietly near the gardens. He desperately wanted to go to her but needed to wait till his mother was in the car ready to go to the burial. She was turning away to join the crowd when he grabbed her hand, pulling her down a side path, he was lost for words to see her. Without speaking a word, she wrapped her arms around his neck, and he held her tight as he let out a sigh of relief.

"I thought I was seeing things when I saw you in the back", he said, slowly letting her out of his embrace but still holding her hands.

"I'm sorry to come uninvited", she whispered.

He smiled and brushed his hand over her cheek fondly.

"Don't be sorry, I need to go, though, please don't leave, will you wait for me?" he pleaded with her softly.

She was so relieved to hear him ask her to stay. "I will".

Stuart squeezed her hands and leant down to kiss her cheek. He walked over to the waiting cars, and she watched them all leave one after the other. The guests mingled in the gazebo for nearly 30 minutes before starting to leave. She walked down a small path, finding a cool spot to sit near a large white fountain. It was nearly an hour later when Stuart found her. He took her hand and held it tightly.

"I'm sorry you have waited so long, will you come with me to the wake?" he asked, holding her hand close to his chest. He looked worn out and defeated. He led her back to the car that his parents were in and opened the backseat door for her. She looked at him, absolutely terrified.

"Claire, this is my mother, Doris, and my father, Keith", he said as they drove away. Both of his parents reached back to shake her hand. He looked across the back seat at her, leant in and whispered in her ear.

"Thank you for coming, Claire".

She felt a hot flush come over her as he held her hand all the way.

The wake was at The Grand Fields Racecourse, in the members stand, and there were a lot of people waiting for them when they arrived. Stuart led her through the room, stopping to hug and thank several people, introducing her to his aunt, Donna, and his sister-in-law before stopping at the bar. He ordered her a glass of red wine and himself a beer, leading her out to the balcony overlooking the track.

"I thought you were heading home with Amy", he said after a long mouthful of beer. He was standing close to her leaning on the handrail, and she rested her hand on his arm.

"She flew home yesterday, and I took a flight here last night, I am sorry to just turn up today, but I really wanted to be here for you", she sipped her wine.

"It was a good surprise, where are you staying?", he asked.

"The Oaklands on Dalton, I got in about 10 last night" she said, smiling.

"You should have called me, Claire, I could have picked you up, you could have stayed with me at my parent's house". He looked at her, suddenly worried that she was staying by herself.

"I didn't want to bother your sister-in-law by ringing to tell you, Michelle sent me the details when I spoke to dad last night and let him know I was going to be away a few more days," she said, taking another sip of her wine.

Leaning into him, she whispered, "I signed over my apartment over to Pia yesterday".

He smiled at her, his deep blue eyes leaping deep into her soul. He put his arm around her waist, pulling her closer to him.

"I fly home tomorrow afternoon".

Stuart finished his beer and faced her. "I need to stay on here for a while and help Mum and Donna tie up some loose ends. I wish I could come home with you tomorrow", he sighed.

Things were wrapping up at the racetrack, Stuart thanked and said goodbye to the last of the guests and by 5pm they were the only ones left. He said goodbye to his parents, letting them know he would follow them home shortly.

"Please let me take you back to the motel, then I will know you are safe", he asked her, his eyes were heavy with grief.

She nodded and he called them a taxi. She sat close to him resting her hand on his knee most of the way back to her hotel.

Claire opened the door to her room, leading him in as he took of his suit jacket. She poured a wine for herself and got him a beer from the mini bar. The sun was going down, she opened the door to the balcony letting in the cool salty breeze.

Claire took off her shoes, sliding down onto the chaise so her head was resting on his shoulder. The tension was high, and they were both drained from the day but happy to be near each other, it felt right.

"What time is your flight tomorrow?" he asked her softly.

"3pm" she replied quietly, playing with his fingers, just like he had done to her's weeks ago.

He watched her take out her earrings.

"Ahh shit," Claire muttered, as one of them became stuck in her hair.

"I've got it," he untangled the earring, leaning over her to put it on the side table. He was so close to her; he could count the freckles on her nose.

She ran her fingers through his beard as he looked down at her. Moving in closer, she looked up and closed her eyes as his warm lips touched hers. She could feel her body tingle down to her toes as he kissed her deeply.

Laying on the couch with him she rested her head on his chest. It must have been an hour later that they were still laying there just holding each other.

"I don't want to move", she whispered.

"I want to stay more than you will ever understand, but I can't, I need to be at home with my family tonight", he laughed suddenly, "I told Mum I was just taking you back to your motel and wouldn't be long, oops", he rolled over so he was looking down at her. "Thank you for everything today, it really means the world to me". "I don't want to leave you here with the idea that this didn't mean something, if you know what I mean". He brushed the hair away from her face and kissed the end of her nose. "I will try to get home as soon as I can", he said, sitting up and reaching for his jacket.

Doing up his jacket buttons, he sat beside her.

"You look beautiful in that dress", he said touching her cheek. With a deep sigh he hung his head. "I don't want to go and leave you here alone".

"I will be fine, I'll have a shower and get an early night", she assured him.

"I promise I will go and buy a new phone tomorrow so I can keep in touch with you". He walked with her to the door. He kissed her again, and then again, trying to leave. He sighed heavily.

"I'll see you soon then". He wrapped his arms around her and held her tightly then kissed her nose. "Goodnight, pretty girl", he said softly as he closed the door behind him.

Chapter 11

Billy and Amy picked Claire up from Reffshore airport the next afternoon. Claire was tired and a little bit lovesick. Amy explained to Claire that she had told Bill about dad's surprise birthday party, and he was in on the plan completely.

"It will be easier to keep it a secret if you have it in town, just tell him you are gonna go for tea for his birthday but fail to mention the 40 people coming to have tea too", he chuckled. "He is gonna be pissed you know", Billy continued, trying to look serious.

"Yes, I imagine he will at first", Amy said smugly.

An hour later they pulled through the entrance gums and parked out front of the homestead. Bobby slowing wobbling out to meet them.

Davis was waiting on the porch and greeted them with a big hug.

"How was your trip?" he asked, "Everything settled with your place?"

Claire kissed her dad on the cheek. "All done, you're stuck with me now", she said, wrapping her arms around his neck.

"I wouldn't have it any other way", he held her tightly.

"How was Melbourne?" he asked her as they stood on the verandah.

"It was sad, but I am glad I went, Stuart seemed happy to see me", she walked inside.

Michelle and Terry listened to Claire as she told them about the surprise party for dad. Michelle looked at her, concerned.

"It's very hard to keep secrets from your dad, he always seems to figure things out".

Claire chewed the inside of her lip. "I know, but we are determined to make it happen, if you can add anyone to this list to invite, I'd really appreciate it". She gave the list to Michelle.

"Amy and I will pop into town tomorrow and talk to Sandy at The Royal and see the bakery for a cake order", Claire said closing the folder in front of her.

"Sounds like you have it sorted, three weeks to go, fingers crossed he doesn't catch wind of it" Michelle said with a half grin.

Claire dragged herself into bed and snuggled down under her thick, soft quilt. Her phone rang at 9.45pm. She leapt across the bed grabbing it as she hit the floor with a loud thud.

"Hello", she said struggling to get up.

"Hey, pretty girl", Stuart said softly. "You ok?", he asked.

"I'm fine, I just fell off the bed,"

Stuart laughed. "I can't talk long, I was just ringing so you have my new number," he said quietly. "I'm sorry, but I don't think I'll be home as soon as I'd hoped, Mum needs me to help her sort out my brother's house", he sighed.

"It's ok, you take as much time as you need, I'm not going anywhere", she said with a heavy heart. She wanted to see him again so desperately. She told him about the plan for Davis's birthday and what they had planned.

"Sounds great, reckon he will figure it out though", Stuart said sternly. "He is a bugger like that, just when you think you have the upper hand".

"It will be on the 25th", she said hoping he would be back by then.

"I'll try my best to be back by then, I've got to go, I'm sorry, I wish I could talk longer. I'll text you in the morning", he said gently.

"I'm looking forward to seeing you", she stuttered with a lump building in her throat.

"Me too, bye pretty girl", he hung up as she fell back on the bed clutching the phone tightly and letting out a deep sigh.

Claire zipped up her jacket a little bit higher as she looked out across the paddock that morning. The breeze was cold, and low grey clouds hung on the sky like giant cotton balls. She carried the bucket of scraps down to the chickens and tossed them over the fence. She didn't have the patience for that damn rooster this morning. Her phone vibrated and after a boxing match with her pocket she managed to get it free.

"Good morning, beautiful, I hope you have a good day". Stuart sent her the same message every morning, the day was not complete without it. It felt like they had come together more since the funeral. He rang her every night as well as texts over the day. She had been writing him letters and putting them in a shoe box to give him when he got back. It had been 8 months since she came home and even though they were not officially a couple she felt like she couldn't go back to life without him.

Terry and Billy picked her up from the homestead and they left for a day of fencing.

"That bag better be full of food", Billy commented, already starving.

"Of course." She squeezed into the middle seat between them.

The morning flew by quickly and before she knew it lunch time had rolled around. She sat on the tray, with the boys sitting on the grass below.

"How is the party planning going?" Terry asked, stuffing a whole sandwich into his mouth.

"I think it's on track, so far, I don't think dad knows", she smiled warily.

"He will not say anything, just pretend he doesn't know while watching everyone plan it around him thinking he doesn't know and all along he does".

Claire laughed, but knew he was right. This is the type of thing her father did, and he would be enjoying the fact that everyone thinks they have got it past him.

"Well, he has not said or done anything to make it seem that he knows, guess I'll see when it comes time for dinner", she said looking concerned.

A few weeks later and the surprise birthday party for Davis had crept up quickly. Billy and Terry were unable to help with so many jobs to do on the farm and Stuart still away, even though Davis had hired a couple of casual workers to help them catch up.

Davis, despite being bald, was stronger than ever. He was now finished his chemo and due for his scans next week to see if the chemo had helped shrink the tumour enough for surgery.

Michelle was right. It had proved difficult to keep the party a secret, Claire was pretty sure he was on to them. Amy and Claire had told him they were taking him to town for dinner Friday night for his birthday in hope that he would think that was what they were hiding. He seemed pretty happy to go, so that was a start.

Claire and Amy waited till dad left with the new casual workers before they left for town. Claire had posted the package of decorations that she and Amy had ordered to Graeme Donaldson's house, luckily he was more than happy to oblige. Keeping secrets in a small town was fun but challenging. The private dining room at The Royal Hotel was quite large. The walls were mustard yellow and the bottom third was wood panelling. It looked like the typical hotel with three-tone carpet and the ever-present smell of stale beer. Sandy, the publican, was a skinny, tattoo-covered woman with blonde hair. She spoke with a whiney voice and her jeans were so tight they should have cut her circulation off. She was nice, though, just a little rough around the edges. Sandy agreed to Amy and Claire keeping the keys to the separate dining room as it was only used for special occasions. They were determined not to have the surprise ruined. They used the large round tables the pub had in the storage room and arranged the chairs around them neatly.

Amy opened the box Graeme had bought in and took out the decorations. The tables had black tablecloths, across the centre of the tables she spread out a circle of silver sequin material and the centre decoration was a silver top hat and a black top hat resting on stands so one sat higher than the other. Amy sprinkled silver table scatters while Claire and Sandy set out the glasses, plates, and cutlery. The room was coming together well. Sandy offered some black chair covers to finish the look off.

"I'm impressed, girls, might have to hire you as event coordinators", Sandy offered. Claire and Amy took the rubbish out to the skip and set off home. The party was tomorrow night and the only thing left to do was the balloons and the cake.

"I'm really proud of the room, we did good", Amy said on the drive home.

"How many are coming?" Claire asked.

Amy looked through the RSVP list. "46, including all of us", Amy stated. "Uncle George is coming but won't get into town till dark", Amy said. "I know Dad hasn't seen Uncle George for 7 years so that will be a great surprise".

Claire chuffed and stared out the window as Amy babbled on.

"Hello, Earth to Claire", she said loudly.

"Sorry", she said as she refocused.

"Have you heard from him?" Amy asked her.

"Yeah a few calls and texts", Claire sighed.

"You really do have feelings for him, don't you?" Amy looked at her while watching the road.

"I miss him." she said quietly.

They turned up the drive to see Terry and one of the new workers slashing the front paddocks. They pulled up in front of the homestead and Claire looked down the lane towards the Grove Cottage where Stuart lived. No cars.

"He will be here", Amy said, rubbing her on the shoulder as they walked into the house. Amy had become quite invested in her sister's feelings and felt her anguish every time she looked at her phone.

Michelle and Davis were in the kitchen. Claire looked through the glass panel in the top of the door to see Michelle stirring a pot on the stove with her father standing behind her with his arms around her waist.

Amy come belting down the hallway, Claire grabbed her by the shirt to stop her from going into the kitchen. Both girls looked through the glass of the kitchen door.

"I knew it", Claire said victoriously.

"I had my suspicions also," Amy pushed the door open and pretended not to see them. Davis casually took a seat on the bar stool against the bench leaving Michelle looking flushed.

"Where have you girls been?" Davis asked. Amy carried a box of cake making supplies and gave them to Michelle.

"They were shopping for birthday cake stuff for me", she said with a wink at Amy and Claire. "And now you have gone and seen it and so now you know," Michelle was maybe a little over exaggerating. Davis smiled and looked inside.

"Better be chocolate", he said as he hugged both of his daughters and excused himself to watch the football in the lounge.

"Michelle, you're a genius, he seemed to have bought that", Amy said with a smug grin. Claire watched him leave the room.

"He knows, I don't know how but he knows, I can feel it in my bones", Claire said doubtfully.

The next afternoon, Sandy set the balloons up as Claire had instructed, around the edge of the room in floating bunches of six both silver and black. The bakery delivered the cake late that afternoon. Claire heard her phone beep at 4pm. The text message from Sandy read,

"Ready to go". Claire smiled and started the rehearsed roleplay she and Amy had discussed with everyone.

"Michelle, instead of you cooking, maybe we should go into the pub tonight for a counter meal since its dad's birthday and all", Amy said with a smile.

"That sounds like a great idea, what do you think Billy?" she asked with a practiced smile.

"Yeah, I could definitely go for some pub grub", he said standing up. "I'll go get changed", he stated loudly, leaving the room.

Davis sat on the couch watching them feeling quite amused at their antics. Claire stood also.

"I have not been out anywhere for tea since being home, what do you think, Dad?" She asked her father.

Davis laughed under his breath. It was the tackiest theatre performance he had ever seen. "Well, I guess it's decided then, dinner in town it is", Davis said rolling his eyes. "Better iron me a shirt, Michelle", he said grumbling up the stairs.

Claire and Amy took off to their rooms to get changed. Michelle stood looking at Terry who had not said a single word the entire time.

"He knows, doesn't he?" he said to Michelle with a frown. She smiled and shrugged as she walked upstairs to iron Davis a shirt.

Claire stood in front of the mirror. She was wearing a navy dress that was tight and stopped at the knee, showing her figure beautifully. Her long curly hair hung down her back freely and she wore nude-pink strappy high heels. Taking a deep breath, she finished her makeup and headed downstairs. Amy wore a nice pair of black jeans, a black and red floral shirt with matching pair of red wedges and was looking forward to meeting up with a new guy she had been seeing.

They drove into town. Michelle drove Davis, Jamie, and Terry in the property 4x4 with *November* written clearly up the side. Davis was looking quite the catch, in a blue-check collared shirt, his good pair of jeans and Durango boots. He wore a baseball cap as he had no hair and wasn't very confident being bald yet. Claire took off her big heels and drove her little blue car with Amy and Billy. Michelle decided it was best that she refuel her car before going to dinner in case the servo would be shut when they finished and to buy the girls some time. The guests were enjoying a drink when Claire announced to the main bar that her guests should proceed into the dining room as her father would arrive soon.

It was hustle and bustle, but everyone was in, and the doors were closed. Billy stood inside the door with his hands ready on the light switch. Sandy gave the thumbs up, and the pub returned to normal. Davis arrived ten minutes later and was met by his daughters in the main bar. Sandy, playing her role as planned, told them they were serving meals in the banquet dining room as there had been a water leak in the main dining area and the carpet was wet and led them down the wide hallway to the doors.

"Find yourself a table and I'll come back to take your order soon."

Claire was scared, her stomach was churning as Dad opened the dining room door at the exact moment Billy flipped on the lights.

"SURPRISE", came the crowd who was gathered inside. Davis, despite nearly falling off his feet, was quite composed and put his arms around his girls as he walked into the room.

So many familiar faces. "George", Davis yelled as he saw his brother cross the room, catching him in an enormous bear hug. Davis walked around the room and said hello to everyone. He was happy and he couldn't think of a time he felt more loved. Claire scanned the room; she could feel herself suddenly very lonely. She wanted Stuart to be here so badly, and he promised her he would try to be.

Sandy had the meal going quickly, a buffet roast dinner with choice of chicken or beef. Everyone was eating and enjoying themselves.

"I think we can call the evening a success so far," Amy said looking smugly at Michelle as they ate.

"You both did a wonderful job, and the food is good too", Amy said taking another bite of her baked potato.

Claire picked at her food. More shifting it around the plate rather than eating it when Sandy came into the room, leant in and whispered to her father. Claire watched Davis follow Sandy out of the room. Amy was quick to notice too.

"What is going on?" Amy mouthed to Claire across the table. Davis came back into the room, taking his seat, but looking quite nervous. He stood and tapped his beer bottle with a spoon.

"Can I have your attention please", he said loudly. The crowd grew silent.

"It's not often that I am surprised, it's not often that people keep secrets from me, but I fear, even though I suspected something was up, I never thought that this grand party was it." The crowd clapped. "Thank you to my daughters, Claire and Amy, for planning this shindig. You girls did good", he said as the crowd applauded once again. "Thank you to all of you who made the effort to come, some of you travelling quite far for tonight, I feel very privileged to be here amongst you all. To my amazing staff and family who help me keep my dreams alive, and last but not least, thank you to Michelle", he said taking her hand and making her stand up. Claire put her hands to her mouth and a gasp followed across the room.

"A lot of you may not know but Michelle and I have been quietly seeing each other for just over 12 months now."

Amy looked across to Claire throwing her hands up in an I told you so gesture.

"She has seen me at my worst," Davis continued, "My daughters and Michelle have looked after me these last several months and I can't express how much love I have for this woman," Davis said as the crowd clapped again. "I have a confession to make to you all, I also have also been keeping a secret of my own", he said as he looked around the room at a lot of stunned faces.

Claire was on the edge of her seat. Amy looked open mouthed at Claire from across the table with the heavy weight of suspense hanging in the air.

Davis walked Michelle out into the middle of the room in front of everyone. Michelle started to become teary.

"I have been keeping this secret for the last three weeks, I had a good friend who had been in Melbourne recently, stay so much longer than he needed to without talking to anyone in case my plan was discovered", Davis said with a smile at Michelle. Claire hung on the edge of his words, her stomach in knots. He was talking about....

The door to the dining room suddenly opened and there he was, it was Stuart like Claire had never seen him before. He walked across the room and handed Davis a small black box, suddenly the crowd started cheering and a loud whistle came just as quickly as it started, it once again, fell silent.

Davis shook Stuart's hand, faced Michelle, and dropped to one knee as Michelle started to sob.

"Michelle, I am not me without you, will you do me the honour of being the other half of me for the rest of our lives, will you marry me?"

Michelle looked at him in disbelief and nodded a yes as the crowded room erupted into whistles, cheers and clapping so loud the main bar could hear them.

Michelle and Davis held each other as Michelle cried uncontrollably.

"Welcome to our engagement party", Davis said loudly taking a mouth full of his beer.

Amy and Claire, both stunned, congratulated their father and were happy for them. It was nice to know he had found happiness again. Claire moved her attention to the man standing across the room from her. Stuart had shaved his beard off, his hair was cut neatly, and he wore no hat. He walked towards her slowly. He was wearing a deep maroon shirt that was collared and unbuttoned at the top, his tan-coloured moleskin pants and polished brown R.M.Williams boots were perfect. He looked incredibly handsome. She found herself completely mute and fixed to the spot, unable to move.

Stuart shook hands with a few of the guests while slowly making his way to Claire.

"Good evening, Pretty Girl", he said with a smile.

"What have you done?" she asked, touching his smooth chin.

"You don't like it?", he asked with a cheeky smile. With tears in her eyes, she touched the sides of his face.

"I love it!!" Stuart sat beside Claire and had some dinner.

"I've been sitting at Mum's for weeks waiting for the ring to be made, then your dad rang me last week and told me to come straight here, not home, so here I am",

Stuart explained. Amy sat across the table and had her mouth wide open.

"I knew he figured it out, but how the hell? We had been so careful", she said wondering where she could have slipped up.

"I believe he caught wind of it all when the woman making the cake rang the house and left a message on the answering machine", Stuart said.

"Damn", Amy said with a thump of her fist on the table.

"So, he rang Sandy and got her playing both sides of the game and asked me to wait for the ring and it played out just like he planned it to", Stuart said, wiping his mouth with a napkin. "Then you girls threw a party for him which changed the plan for the proposal".

Davis and Michelle stood at the front of the room as she lit the candles on the cake. The crowd joined in to sing happy birthday to Davis as he blew out his candles.

The party went on, the DJ started the music as more and more people danced. Davis looked happy; the happiest Amy had seen him for years. He danced with Michelle in the first slow dance of the evening. Several couples joined them on the dancefloor. Stuart stood up, held his hand out to Claire. "May I have this dance pretty girl?" he said with those deep blue eyes cutting right into her.

Claire took his hand. He led her past the tables and onto the dancefloor. He smelled amazing. His strong arms sat about her waist as she wrapped her arms around his neck. It wasn't unnoticed. Claire and Stuart had more eyes looking at them than Davis and Michelle did, but she didn't care.

"I'm sorry I didn't tell you what was going on", he whispered in her ear.

"It's ok, I couldn't be happier for Dad", she said softly. "He deserves to have someone special in his life, I just wish we had known sooner, must have been hard for them to keep it a secret".

"Think we have all known for quite a while," he said as he held her tighter.

"I've waited so long to have your arms around me", she whispered in his ear.

He smiled at her; his deep blue eyes looked right into her soul.

"I want to kiss you", he said softly. She dug her nails into his back as her stomach churned nervously.

"I want to kiss you too".

Looking around for an escape, he took her hand and led her through the crowded room, down a dimly lit hall and through an ornate set of French doors. The empty balcony that sat at the front of the hotel over the main entrance and footpath below was currently under construction with paint cans and ladders all over the place. The railing along the front of the pub had fairy lights strung along making colourful patterns on the natural stone walls. He took both of her hands and led her down to the far end into the shadows.

"I've missed you", he said softly.

Claire smiled and gently ran her fingertips along his now smooth chin. The music was still playing inside, and they could hear the occasional cheer coming from the party.

"Now, dance with me, Claire?" Stuart said in that deep voice that melted Claire to the core. He took her hands and placed them around his neck, put his hands on her waist and gently they swayed to the music. She rested her cheek against his as they danced in the dark. Running her fingertips along the back of his neck, playing with his blonde curls.

A sudden crack of thunder echoed through the night flickering the fairy lights. As they flickered off and on, the rain started to fall on the tin roof. He ran his hands up her back, over her shoulders into her hair and gently holding her jaw in both hands. Every part of her ached for him, she looked into his deep blue eyes as he hovered his lips over her mouth, kissing her nose before pressing his lips to hers. He kissed her like nothing she had ever experienced, he was strong, and his tongue gently brushed over hers. As he pulled her closer, the kiss became harder, intense, and her legs started to feel like they were going to give way. He kissed each cheek and across to her ear as she softly groaned. He cupped her bum cheeks perfectly in his hands, her legs were trembling as he lifted her off her feet wrapping her legs around his waist, he pressed her up against the brick wall, kissing her neck. She gasped quietly, trying not to make too much noise, pulling herself up and kissing him harder, breathing heavier. He could feel her body gently trembling as she pulled away.

"We can't," she said, breathing heavily she slid down, "Not here".

He pressed his forehead to hers. "Let's go then", he said.

The need to kiss him again was intoxicating. Stuart led her by the hand back inside. Claire found Amy and Billy dancing; she smiled as they came closer.

"We are gonna head home", she said with a shaky voice, handing Amy the keys to her little blue car. The party was loud. Billy stared at Stuart with a cheesy grin.

"Drive careful", she said looking at Stuart.

Amy kissed Claire on the cheek, pointed to her chest and then to hers.

"Don't worry I will tell Dad", Amy said.

"Don't hurt him too much", Billy said under his breath, just loud enough that Claire could hear him, giving him an embarrassed look, they both laughed. Stuart led Claire out to his ute holding the door for her.

The drive home was tense, he leant over and kissed her cheek at every stop, holding her hand and playing with her fingers on his lap, eventually they pulled up at the Grove Cottage. He opened the ute door for her, dropping her shoes on the porch before slipping off his boots and carrying her through the front door. Claire smiled as Stuart leant down to kiss her. This time she could feel the desire between them so strong. As he pressed against her, she could feel every curve of his body. The fire was still going in the lounge, the soft warm glow filled the room as she unbuttoned his shirt, revealing his soft blonde chest hair, she gently kissed his chest as his shirt dropped to the floor. She unbuttoned his jeans and before long he was standing before her naked. He was muscular and sexy. His body was a map of chiselled muscles. She gently ran her hands up his chest as he slipped her dress over her head leaving her standing in the fire glow in just her g-string. Her breasts were round and her nipples hard as he gently ran his thumb over them before laying her down on the sheepskin rug in front of the dancing wood fire.

He nibbled down her neck, as she arched her back with a deep moan, he gently moved his tongue over her nipples. Her breath was getting heavier by the moment, Stuart kissed her stomach and pulled off her black g-string. He kissed her thigh then slowly down further, her legs quivered as she reached down and pushed his face heavier against her before arching her back and gasping suddenly, she could hardly stand it any longer. She reached down and took his thick erection in her hand and gently squeezed, making him let out a deep moan as she tickled his balls. She moved herself on top of him, placing her hands on the floor at his shoulders, she leant down and kissed his nose. She hovered on the tip of his cock, teasing him as he wriggled with anticipation under her. He reached up to hold her breasts, pinching her nipples gently, which was nearly enough to make her lose control, then she let him slip deep inside her. She rocked back and forth slowly, moving her hips in circles. He sat up, leaning against the lounge on the floor facing her as she wrapped her legs around his waist holding her hips against his, she leant her arms back onto the floor moving him in and out slowly. He leant forward to her beautiful round breasts biting her nipples, she let out a groan as he pushed inside her slowly, deeper. He couldn't hold back as he lowered her onto her back and pushed himself into to her faster and harder, they were breathing heavily, moaning loudly as the intensity built quickly. She reached forward holding his firm butt cheeks and dug her nails in just as she reached her limit, he could feel her coming under him, her body shaking. He rolled her over onto her stomach pulling her up to her knees and slid back into her as she let out a near squeal. She grabbed handfuls of sheepskin, breathing and moaning loudly. He reached under her, squeezing her nipple and worked his way down to find her clit, he pushed into her deeper as he came. He didn't stop, but rather slowed down gently, moving himself in and out as she knelt in front of him, rising up so her back was against his chest, her head back on his shoulder. He kissed her neck and nibbled her ear lobes, still rubbing her faster and faster until they both reached an unimaginable climax, her entire body shaking in his hands. They both fell to the floor, legs and arms entangled. He kissed her, brushing his tongue gently across hers and kissed her ear lobe as he wrapped his arms around her tightly. She had never had such mind-blowing, intense sex in her life. She lay in his arms looking up into those deep blue eyes and nothing mattered. She pressed her ear to his chest, listened to his heart beating, watching the fire crackling away, her hair spread across his chest.

"I'm in love with you, Claire", he whispered. She felt a lump grow as she lifted her head to face him, pulling him closer and kissing him again.

Claire woke the next morning, surrounded by a mess of crisp white sheets and pillows that smelled like vanilla.

"Morning, old boy", she said affectionately with a big smile. She was flirting with him, and she couldn't control herself doing so, her heart beat faster every time he looked at her. He rolled over sleepily and snugged his face onto her pillow.

"Good morning, pretty girl", he said as he nibbled her neck. She giggled. While they lay entangled in each other's arms on the floor, she felt safe, but also insecure at the same time. A new wave of fears ran through her mind. Finally, they were here at this point where everything was perfect, a point that she had longed for since returning home and suddenly she was so afraid of losing him.

"Want a coffee?" Stuart asked, sifting through the pillows to find his pants. She lay there, watching him flip the jug on. He was ridiculously handsome without his beard and his muscular back nearly melted her all over the floor. Sitting on the footstool beside her, he put her coffee on the small side table and smiled. Leaning down to gently kiss her lips, he found himself feeling completely content.

"I better head up to the house and check on Dad." She raised her arms up above her head stretching her muscles. Kneeling in front of him wrapped in a sheet, she kissed him again, then took a big mouth full of coffee.

"I'll be up soon, I have to check on a few things first", he said as she pulled her clothes on. She smiled. After another soft kiss, then another, she finally tip-toed down the front path of his cottage and slowly shuffled along the rocky drive carrying her heels back towards the main house.

It felt like the walk of shame when she neared the homestead to find Michelle and Davis sitting on the veranda with steaming cups of coffee. Oh, how mortifying she thought. Busted by her father. She opened the gate and walked across the lawn to them with a sleepy smile, instantly embarrassed. Her hair was in a messy bun on top of her head, she felt and looked like someone who had had a big night rolling in the sheets and the stupid grin her father had on his face didn't help.

"Good morning, Daddy", she said as she kissed his cheek practically sprinting in the door. Davis couldn't help but laugh.

Chapter 12.

Michelle, Claire, and Amy took Davis into Reffshore Hospital the following week to have his scans. Davis, as usual, was not impressed to have so many women fussing over him and was keen to get it over and done with.

Claire and Amy had a coffee in the cafeteria while Michelle waited in the waiting room for him.

"Which one is he?" Claire asked looking around eagerly. Amy was seeing one of the emergency room doctors and had been for a couple of months now.

"That one in the red scrubs", she said looking over her shoulder. It was typical of the sisters to be chatting away like they were in high school again talking about their schoolyard crushes.

"The one coming over?" Claire smirked.

Amy turned just as he slipped up behind her and kissed her cheek.

"Claire this is Tim, Tim this is my sister, Claire." She introduced him as he shook her hand, pulling up a seat beside them. Claire read his name badge. Dr Tim Johnson, Emergency Dept.

"So, your dad's scan is today, how are you both holding up?" he asked, rubbing Amy's leg under the table.

"As good as we can be, I guess", Amy replied.

Claire studied Tim carefully. He was well dressed and presented, he was clean shaven and had ginger red hair. He seemed gentle and calm, exactly the opposite of Amy.

"How has your day been?" Claire asked.

"It's been a long night and pretty busy actually, I'll be off around 3. Do you ladies want to grab a bite to eat tonight at the pub, my shout?" he asked them both as he held Amy's hand.

"We could double date", Amy replied with a huge smile.

Claire suddenly felt uncomfortable and could feel her cheeks going redder by the minute.

"Um, I am not sure", Claire replied hesitantly. Tim checked his watch and lifted his coffee high to drink the last drops.

"Well let me know anyway," Tim said as he gave Amy a gentle hug and a kiss before going back to work.

"He seems really nice, Amy", Claire said approvingly.

"Yeah, he is pretty perfect", Amy sighed. "How are you and Stuart going?", she mused with a cheeky grin.

"Good, he told me he was in love with me the night of dad's party". Claire blushed but looked distant.

"Awwww, that's gorgeous, but I get the feeling there is a 'but' here". Claire looked at Amy and sighed.

"I didn't say it back".

Amy studied her sisters face carefully. "Do you love him?", she asked up front.

Claire smiled, feeling embarrassed. "Yes".

"Well tell him, no regrets", she touched her chest and pointed to Claire.

"I love you too".

The girls chatted about the good doctor Tim until Michelle came down the hall looking puffy eyed.

Claire rose to her feet quickly.

"Are you ok?" she asked Michelle, who sat slowly down beside them.

"They are going to keep Davis in overnight, he had a bit of a turn after the scan and they want to run some tests", Michelle said, her hands shaking.

"What kind of turn?"

Michelle took Amy's hand and rubbed her shoulder in comfort. Claire just sat there, stunned.

"He was fine when we got here", Amy said wiping a tear away.

"The technician said he passed out not long after the scan finished and she couldn't wake him, so called a code blue and the next thing I know, alarms are going off and people are running past me, and they are taking me to another room to tell me it was Davis coding", Michelle said in disbelief.

"The doctor has not given me much info yet but said they would be keeping him over night at least and would speak to us shortly", Michelle said taking both of their hands.

"I want to see him", Claire said sternly standing up.

"Come on, we will all go back up to the waiting room and see what is going on", Amy replied.

The three ladies sat in the waiting room quietly and didn't speak. After a while, Dr Wong came out and called for them to go into a small office down the hall.

Dr Wong sat in front of them with a serious look and proceeded to explain in detail what had happened.

"Mr Gannon has had a stroke, which you may already know is where the blood flow to the brain has been interrupted, it happened after his scan today, the technician called a code blue which resulted in Mr Gannon needing resuscitation", he said trying to keep it simple. Claire had her hand to her mouth in shock while Amy was openly crying.

"Where is he, can we see him?" Amy struggled to speak.

"Mr Gannon is in Ward B and is awake and aware of his surroundings, there seems to be no memory loss or paralysis at this stage, but I do want him to stay so I can do some blood tests and review the scans."

Michelle was calm and composed.

"Can we see him?" she asked politely.

"Yes, that should be ok. I'll have the nurse show you where to go, but I suggest keeping the visits short and one at a time. He needs to stay calm; he is a bit sleepy." He instructed.

Dr Wong opened the door and briefly spoke to the nurse who escorted them down the stairs and into Ward B.

"You go in first", Michelle said to Amy "Claire and I will wait here in the hall."

Claire wrapped her arms around Michelle.

"He will be fine", Michelle said, hiding her concern as best she could.

"I think I will stay here tonight, though, I should give the house a call and let everyone know what is happening." Michelle took her phone from her bag.

"No, I'll do it, you wait and go in next", Claire said. Michelle put her phone away. Claire walked down the hall and sat by a large window looking out into the children's ward gardens and dialled Stuart's number.

"Hey, pretty girl", he said as he always did when she called. Hearing his voice, she burst into tears telling him about what had happened. "Oh, shit, I'll let the boys know when they get back from the paddocks, I'll come into town soon", he was genuinely concerned. "I will bring a few things for Michelle and your dad if you like".

"Michelle said she was going to stay the night with him so a change of clothes would be great".

Amy was waiting in the hall when Claire returned. She held her sister tightly as she cried. Amy was the emotional one of the sisters and openly showed her feelings when she was upset or in trouble.

"He will be ok", Claire said wiping her sister's teary cheeks as Michelle came back out into the hall.

"They are going to let me stay with him tonight, he wants to see you, Claire", she said. Clearly, she had been crying.

Claire walked forward, hesitating briefly, then with a sigh pushed the door handle down and walked into the room. Davis was laying quietly with the blankets pulled right up to his chin. He had oxygen prongs in his nose and had his eyes closed.

"Daddy?", she whispered taking his hand. He slowly opened his eyes and smiled at her. She sat down and rested her head on his shoulder. Davis pushed the blankets down to reveal the electrodes still stuck to his chest. He patted her head gently.

"I'm fine, don't you worry", he reassured her in a croaky voice.

Claire lifted her head and smiled at him.

"You better be, I don't want to lose you yet", she said holding his hand tightly. Davis, despite looking tired, huffed.

"You're not getting rid of me that easy, girl".

He was always a shit stirrer and making light of situations. She held his hand for a while as he closed his eyes again. She kissed him on the cheek.

"I love you, Daddy, I'll be back in the morning, ok".

He nodded without opening his eyes and she left the room.

Michelle gave Claire the keys to the car.

"I'll be fine here, you drive the car back home", she said. "Bring me back a change of clothes in the morning?" Michelle asked.

"I spoke to Stuart a while ago, he is going to bring you and Dad a few things, he should be here soon", Claire gave Michelle a hug and took the keys as Tim came up the hallway and scooped Amy up into a long embrace.

Michelle quietly slipped back into Davis's room as they all started to walk back down the hallway towards the foyer.

"I'm going to stay at Tim's tonight", Amy said with Tim's arm around her. Claire nodded and handed Amy the keys to the car. They came down the wide stairs to find Stuart sitting in the foyer. He stood as they came closer.

Amy hugged Stuart briefly, introduced him to Tim, said goodbye to everyone, and then they left for Tim's place.

Stuart didn't hesitate and wrapped his arms around Claire. She wanted to sit down on the floor and break down, she wanted to burst into tears and scream, she wanted to run as fast as she could outside, but she didn't, she held her composure, taking the backpack of clothes and toiletries for Michelle, Stuart waited while she ran them back to the room. He held Claire's hand as they walked to his ute.

The afternoon had clouded over and turned cold.

"Do you want to get some dinner in town before we head home?" Stuart asked her carefully.

"Maybe we should and take it home for all of us to have. I'm sure Terry and Bill will be hungry", she said as he got in the cab beside her.

"That's a good idea".

A few hours later, Claire and Stuart turned through the entrance gums into *November*. Terry and Bill met them at the gate concerned for Davis. Passing the groceries out to Bill she slid down from the passenger door.

The four of them sat at the table, eating hot chicken and gravy rolls, and talked about what had happened that morning. The mood was sombre. Terry and Bill both went to bed after dinner leaving Claire to wash up the few dishes. Stuart stood behind her, his arms around her waist with his chin sitting on her shoulder. She rested her head back to lean on his shoulder before turning to face him, she had not said anything when he told her he was in love with her, she was afraid to say the words out loud. Sitting beside her father today, seeing how quickly life can change, she realised she couldn't let herself be afraid anymore, she wanted to be happy, moving back home was the first step to mending her broken heart and in a lot of ways, letting Stuart go was one of the biggest mistakes she ever made. She had never stopped loving Stuart and she had waited 10 years to be here at this point.

"I love you too". She whispered.

Chapter 13

Billy and Terry left early that morning. Despite everything, the paddocks still needed to be ready to seed in a few weeks and that meant hours on the tractor. With Davis out of action, it seemed more desperate now to get the work done. Jamie pulled his ute in, and Bill updated him on Davis.

Claire sat on the porch drinking her coffee, watching the fog start to life from mountains in the distance. So many things were going through her mind, it felt like it could explode at any moment. She was worried about her father. She was not ready to lose him. Bobby nuzzled his cold, wet nose into her arm for a head scratch, promptly dropping himself at her feet, all four legs in the air. She smiled at the old dog's antics, giving him a good belly scratch. The door opening behind her made her jump.

"You ok?" Stuart asked as he sat beside her. She rested her head on his shoulder and sighed.

"Yeah, I'm ok".

"When you're ready I can run you into town" he said gently leaning his cheek against her head. Davis had been in hospital for three days and was getting more restless by the minute. Michelle had called last night to tell them he would, more than likely, be home the next day.

The drive in was quiet. Claire stared out the window through most of the trip, deep in thought. Stuart pulled into the carpark.

"I can't come in, I need to do some jobs in town, your father is going to ask me about them, and I need to be able to tell him he has nothing to worry about" he said shortly. He kissed her cheek and she agreed to call him with any news.

Amy was sitting in with Dad when Claire knocked on the door. Michelle was having a shower. Dad was sitting up in a chair beside his bed eating his breakfast. He looked cheery and a lot more alert than the first time she saw him.

"Hey, Daddy", she said as she kissed his cheek. She sat on the bed beside him looking at his breakfast tray.

"I'm eating, don't you start on me too", he said sarcastically. Claire smiled and laughed.

"Nice to see you back to normal", she looked at him amused.

"They are ready to get rid of him now, he whinges too much", Amy said laughing.

Davis looked at both of his daughters and rolled his eyes. Michelle came in and took a seat at the end of the bed, drying her hair.

"Hopefully, you can come home soon", Amy noted.

"The doctors doing the morning rounds should pop in soon", Michelle said, repeating what the nurses told her outside.

A gurgling sound loudly announced that Davis had finished his juice and he dropped the empty carton on his tray.

"I could go a decent bloody coffee", he said abruptly.

Amy rolled her eyes and stood up, assuring him that she would go and grab him a cappuccino from the hospital café. She kissed his cheek and off she went. Dr Wong came in an hour later.

"I hear you're keen to leave us", he commented as he took a seat at the end of the bed looking through his night chart. "You have had a stroke, Mr Gannon, not a massive one but enough to give everyone a scare", he said without looking up from his papers. "I will send you home today, but only under the care of these ladies and on the condition that you don't overdo it, no tractor work, no heavy exertion, and most importantly, no stress", he said firmly.

Davis didn't look amused at all.

"I trust these ladies will have you resting, I want to see you back on Friday for a follow up," he said looking at Michelle and Claire.

"I can guarantee he will be resting", Claire said, looking sternly at her father.

Davis looked like a child who had had his PlayStation taken away, pouting his lips, and folding his arms in protest.

As soon as Dr Wong left, Davis was up and fussing in the bed side draws to get his clothes.

"That's it, I'm ready, let's go", he said triumphantly as Michelle packed the last of his toiletries into his bag. A knock sounded at the door and Amy and Tim walked in.

"I see you are ready to go, Davis, didn't take you long", Tim smiled as Amy raised an eyebrow, introducing her father to Tim.

"I know who he is, Amy, I've met him before, I'm one ahead of you my girl", he said to a confused Amy. Tim shook Davis's hand firmly.

"Nice to see you again," Amy looked at her father, about to open her mouth to ask.

"I actually had the pleasure of watching the footy last night during my break with your dad in the staff room", he chuckled.

"Was a bloody good game", Davis thought with a big grin. "Pity you back the wrong team, mate", he laughed again tapping Tim on the shoulder with a friendly shove.

"The staff room, Dad?", Claire asked.

"Was the only tv in the place that had the game on, don't worry, the nurse let me".

"I'm sure in the end she had no choice" Michelle muttered to herself.

Leaving his room, they walked down the wide stairs into the foyer.

"Tim and I are going camping for a few days, Dad", she said giving him a hug.

"Yep, I know". He said smugly. Amy looked open-mouthed at Tim.

"What else have you both been talking about?" she questioned Tim with her hands perched on her hips. Tim shook Davis's hand again and winked.

"Have a good time", Michelle said as they walked away.

"Do you want to come back with us, Claire?", she asked.

"I am going to wait in town for a while until Stuart is ready and I'll come home with him", Claire said giving her father a hug. Davis looked suspiciously at his daughter.

"Is there something we need to talk about later?" he asked his daughter firmly. She smiled.

"I'll see you later, Daddy", Claire said as she left the carpark and walked towards the main street.

The sunshine was lovely and warm as Claire walked along the main street of Reffshore. The shops were all open and had displays out on the foot path for passers-by to see. It was a pretty town with wide roads, typical of regional towns, lined with tall trees. She felt relieved and happy knowing her father was on the way home.

"Well, hello there", she heard a voice behind her. It was Lisa Donaldson coming from a vintage homewares shop. She greeted her with a friendly hug.

"How is your dad going? I heard he wasn't well", she asked kindly. The joys of a small town, everyone knew everyone's business and most of the time knew things before you even did.

"He is doing much better, thank you. He's on the way home as we speak," Claire said proudly.

"Do you have time for a coffee so we could have a chat?" Lisa asked. With a smile Claire nodded, and they walked around the corner into Maxie's Café, finding a table near the window.

"So, I've been meaning to call you, I have a massive favour to ask you, but by all means, don't feel pressured to say yes." Lisa continued, "I have no one to teach a year 11 Advanced English class for next term, I am desperate, and I know Advanced English was one of your preferred classes." Lisa held her hands together like she was praying.

Claire scrunched her face up in despair.

"Wow, I'm definitely keen to teach Advanced English it's one of my favourite subjects", Claire thought carefully. "Can I have some time to think about it?".

"Oh, absolutely. There is no rush, we have 6 weeks till I would need to have a definite answer, but I wanted to give you the chance before I advertised it. Not that I would get the interest that I hope for I'm afraid." Lisa said scooping the last of the milky foam from her cup. "It's hard finding committed teachers in the bush".

Claire took a sip of her coffee. It was strange how things in her life were starting to fall together. Lisa and Claire chatted quietly for another half an hour before Claire noticed Stuart's ute across the street at the rural supply store.

"I'm sorry to be rude, Lisa, but I really need to get going," she said, giving Lisa a hug goodbye.

"I'll be hearing from you then?" Lisa said hopefully.

"I will definitely be in touch".

The bell rang loudly as Claire opened the door of Evan and Sons Rural Services.

"Afternoon, Claire", Bradley said as she leant on the counter. Bradley was in the same year as Claire at school and she knew him well.

"Hey, Brad, what's new?" she said, looking up to see Stuart through the window in the office behind him. Stuart, with his back to her, was talking to a blonde woman she didn't know. She was laughing and playing with her hair before reaching over and touching his arm.

"How is your dad? I heard he was not well", Brad asked.

Claire was half listening to him but was fixed on Stuart through the window.

"Yeah, he is doing much better thanks. Hey, who is that with Stuart?" she asked, tilting her head behind him.

"Oh, that's Sarah, she is new", he said without any thought.

She saw Stuart stand and he shook Sarah's hand and kissed her on the cheek. Coming out past Brad he smiled when he saw Claire standing at the counter. Sarah came to stand beside Brad, taking a printed receipt from the printer and handing it to Stuart to sign.

Sarah smiled at Claire. Stuart put his arm around her.

"Sarah, this is my girlfriend, Claire Gannon, Davis's eldest daughter."

Sarah stretched out her hand to shake Claire's.

"Pleased to meet you", Claire said, smiling.

"I'll be back in a few days to grab that part. Thanks, Sarah, catch you later, Brad", Stuart said taking Claire's hand leaving the store and Brad looking surprised.

Claire paused as he opened the door of the ute for her.

"You ok?" he asked as she stood there staring.

"You introduced me as your girlfriend", she said with a smile.

Stuart took a step towards her, leant down and kissed her without hiding anything, in plain sight of the street. Her body felt like it could explode.

"Well, can I call you my girlfriend?"

She smiled, grabbed him by the shirt and kissed him again.

It was the first time in weeks that Davis had everyone back at *November* for dinner. He took great pleasure in cooking the BBQ and it wasn't long before the entire family was sitting together on the verandah talking about their days.

Michelle, Amy and Tim, Jamie and his Girlfriend Shannon, Billy, Terry, and Claire and Stuart. This was Davis's family. They may not all be blood related but everyone at the table were the ones he loved most.

Stuart held Claire's hand under the table and played with her fingers. He felt happy, completely content.

Clearing his throat loudly, Davis stood up.

"Just wanted to share a little news with you all, Michelle and I have already applied for our marriage licence, and we have decided that we don't want to wait and would like to have a small ceremony here next month on the 15th".

"Cheers to that," Terry said raising his glass.

"Cheers", everyone raised their glasses to toast.

"Dad, that's 3 weeks away", Amy was in a moment of shock. "3 weeks to organise a wedding, it's ok, it can be done, I got this". Amy was convincing herself anxiously.

Claire stood up from the table and walked into the house. Pouring herself another wine she stood in the kitchen staring at the calendar on the fridge.

"Are you ok?", Billy said quietly as Michelle came in with some glasses. Claire smiled and nodded.

"Amy and Tim have gone back into town", she said, washing the glasses and putting them in the dishrack. "I think Tim is a lovely boy", Michelle stated.

"Yes, I like him", Claire smiled. "She looks happy, and that's all that matters".

"I'm heading to bed, night guys", Billy kissed Claire on the cheek and headed for the bunk house.

She drunk the last of the wine and finished the washing up, she could see Davis and Stuart out the kitchen window.

Davis moved a few chairs down to sit beside Stuart as the ladies went inside.

"I've had time lately to think about when my time comes," Davis started. "We have known each other for a long time, Brother", he said slapping Stuart on the shoulder fondly.

"Yes, we have".

"So, you love my daughter?". He didn't shy away from being honest and at times his tact landed him in trouble. Stuart knew he would eventually have to have this conversation, but he found it very difficult to talk about Claire without becoming emotional.

"Yes sir, I do". Stuart looked Davis right in the eyes and found himself choking up.

"Promise me, you know, just in case, that you will look after her when I'm gone".

"I promise".

Davis looked at his friend getting emotional.

"I want to ask you for your permission, for Claire's hand, you know, just in case". Davis wiped a tear from his cheek, stood up and gave Stuart a firm handshake and nodded his approval.

Chapter 14

Davis sat patiently in the waiting room. Claire poured herself a plastic cup of cold water from the cooler. Dad decided he wanted to come in for his follow up with no fuss so only bought Claire with him. Dr Wong was quiet when they were called into the surgery.

"Take a seat", he said as he motioned them to the chairs in front of his desk. Claire watched his face as he read over the notes he had written on the top of the pile of paperwork before bringing up a picture on his computer, turning the screen around so they could see it. Claire knew exactly what she was looking at and after a quick glance at Dad she rested her hand on his knee.

"Mr Gannon, we have seen each other several times since the start of the year and come to know each other well, you have had four rounds of chemo, you had a small stroke when you came for your scan, which you have recovered from well at this stage. I have carefully studied your PET and MRI scans that were taken last week and unfortunately, we have not been successful at shrinking the tumours in your lungs, however, it has not increased in size either." Dr Wong flicked through several images before turning the screen around again.

"Unfortunately, we have also discovered secondary lesions here in the Cerebrum", he said pointing to the diagram he held for them to see. "These are known as Metastatic lesions and there are four of them which are quite small, I'm sorry I could not have given you better news today."

Claire felt like she weighed five ton. She sat up strait and cleared her throat.

"What treatments are there?" Davis asked quietly.

Claire, with her hand over her mouth in shock, knew deep down, what was about to come out of his mouth.

"These tumours are Metastatic, which again means they are secondary to the original diagnosis of lung cancer, and they are inoperable, I'm afraid. I'm sorry, Mr Gannon, but we can't offer any treatment now. We will be more focussed on managing the symptoms and keeping you as comfortable as possible through palliative care".

Claire slumped heavily back into her chair. "How long do we have?"

"I have arranged a meeting for after we finish here with the palliative care team here who can talk you through the options you may like to explore, I can also forward you to a counsellor. I know this is difficult news. As for a time frame, I think we are looking at up to 3 months."

Dr Wong, despite his usually terrible bedside manner, was considerate when delivering the news and stayed with Claire and Davis until the palliative care team were ready for them. Davis shook the doctor's hand as he and Claire sat down.

The drive home was silent as usual. Dad snored loudly in the passenger seat as she pulled between the entrance gums. Billy, Terry, and Jamie sat along the bench against the wall of the dining room while Claire, Amy, Stuart, and Michelle sat at the table with Dad as the news was delivered to the room.

"I ain't dead yet, though, so don't go crying and fussin'. There are crops to look after" Davis said, standing up and putting his hat on. "Come on you lot", he said looking at Billy, Jamie, and Terry.

Michelle had been through cancer before with her late husband and knew what was to come.

"I know this is hard for you girls, but there are a few things we need to think about while he has the ability to make decisions. We will need to go over his Will and..."

Amy burst into tears and ran from the room.

"I'm sorry, Claire", Michelle said wiping a tear from her cheek.

"I know what you are saying and you're right, but right now, I can't deal with that, I am going to go check on Amy", Claire touched Michelle on the shoulder as she left the room.

Claire walked down the verandah and through the gate in the fence. Walking along the steppingstones, she found Amy sitting on a wooden bench on the edge of the white pebble circle at their mum's grave. The garden bed the girls had planted was starting to grow thick with flowers and a bottle brush tree in the middle was flowering.

"Hey there", Claire softly wrapped her arms around Amy's neck from behind, resting her chin on her shoulder. "Are you ok?"

"I'm sorry, I needed some air". Amy held several white pebbles in her hands, moving them around to make a quiet grinding noise. "I've been thinking about Dad, I think we should try to make the wedding as big and beautiful as we can".

"That sounds really nice, Amy".

"He is going to leave us; I want to make sure we make these next few months as happy as we can for him".

Claire sat down beside her sister and there it was, as if nearly on cue, a scent of lavender filled the air.

"See, Mum agrees".

Michelle and Davis's wedding day came around quickly. Claire and Amy had planned the entire wedding in three weeks. They stood inside the white marquee on the side lawn of the homestead. The wedding was tomorrow, and they had managed to send Michelle away for an overnight getaway with her sister at a boutique spa so they could set up and surprise her.

Stuart had taken Davis into town to pick up their suits. Peace at last with no distractions.

The ceremony was set up under a big gum tree in the house yard with an arch and rows of white chairs in front.

The reception marquee had clear walls and a draped ceiling. Jamie and Terry put together the tables arranging them around the centre dance floor while Billy was stringing fairy lights across the roof. Amy set up the bar. It was a long haybale construction with old, paint peeling doors as the bar. The band was set up on the side of the dance floor.

"It looks amazing", Claire said as she put the centrepieces on each table. The colour theme was navy, gold, and burgundy. Each table had navy painted jars of various shapes and sizes each with burgundy flowers, and gold menus and place cards. Claire and Amy had spent three days painting all the jars collected from the op shops, neighbours, and family.

"It's perfect".

"Where do you want these?" Billy said, carrying in another box of wine glasses.

"Just over near the bar, thanks Bill", Claire unpacked the wine for the tables and loaded the beer cans into an old bathtub, which tomorrow would be filled with ice. Claire heard a car pull up on the gravel out front and looked up to see Uncle George standing at the marquee doors.

"Well, good afternoon", George said as a very excited Amy wrapped her arms around his neck. He leant over and kissed Claire on the cheek and shook Billy's hand.

"Doesn't this look amazing?" He said looking around. "I've got three wine barrels in the truck if you strong fellas want to get them out", he said throwing his keys to Terry as he and Jamie went past.

"So, where is the groom this fine afternoon?".

"Stuart has taken him into town to pick up the suits, they should be back soon", Claire replied.

George, with a sudden serious look on his face turned to her. "How is he going, seriously?"

Claire sighed heavily.

"For now, there isn't much change, Uncle, he has been cheery and trying to hide his feelings. He has been a bit forgetful but not too bad", she said putting knives and forks on the tables.

Jamie and Terry rolled in the giant wine barrels.

"Where do you want these, Claire?".

"Around the side of the bar, thanks, guys", she said.

"Brother!" Roared Davis and he and Stuart walked into the marquee, greeting George in a giant bear hug.

"How bout us blokes head into town to the pub for dinner", George suggested

It was nearly midnight when Stuart watched from the door as Claire put the last of nearly 300 the tea light candles around the room, hundreds of fairy lights twinkled as she looked over their work. It was done.

Smiling when she saw him, she fell into his arms, breathing in that sweet smelling aftershave. She turned the switch and the marquee fell into darkness. Stuart took her hand as she walked past him.

"I've missed you". She looked up into his eyes. She had missed him so much in the last week, they had barely seen each other leading up to the wedding. Stuart worked hard to get the farm work done and with the wedding list of things to do they were both so busy.

"Do you want to come and stay with me tonight?"

Claire smiled and sighed hard. "I want to, but I think I should stay here with Amy tonight. It's going to be a long day tomorrow".

He kissed her gently goodnight as she walked in and closed the door.

Chapter 15

Mother nature had delivered the morning of the wedding, it was a beautiful day. Claire, with her hair in rollers, walked around the marquee putting the final touches on the tables and tying gold sashes around the chairs. The smell of the spit roast pork outside was making her drool. Amy, also with her hair in rollers, walked around with Tim, showing him their work.

"It really does look fantastic; you both should be proud". He said looking at the old clawfoot bathtub full of beer. "I think this is my favourite part, however", he said with a cheeky smile. "I have not seen your dad today".

"Dad and his groomsman have gone into town for shaves and cuts", Claire said from across the table. "Which is good, cause it keeps them out of the way". She smiled.

Claire and Amy were bridesmaids, Alice, Michelle's sister, was maid of honour. Davis had George as his best man, Stuart, and Billy on his side.

"Grab yourself a beer, Tim, Amy and I have to go finish getting ready".

"I'll see you in a few hours". Amy said kissing Tim several times before Claire dragged her upstairs.

Michelle was having her hair done in the lounge room, the hair and makeup artists had been going for a few hours. Amy sat for her makeup followed by Claire. A jolly young man in a floral shirt, suit pants and a bold red bow tie knocked on the door. It was Angus Franklin the photographer.

"Hello, ladies," he said as he came in with an enormous smile and friendly demeanour. He floated around, taking photos. Alice looked out the window to see guests arriving.

120 people filed in over the next half hour taking their seats at the ceremony site. The caterers were busy handing the guests some light refreshments.

Davis, George, Stuart, and Billy stood at the end of the aisle looking smart in their navy suits and burgundy ties. Bobby, dad's faithful black lab sat under the tree. Davis looked happy as he gazed out over the guests. The music started, Claire and Amy walked down the aisle first, their burgundy dresses gently touching the grass as they moved forward. Davis came forward and kissed his daughters and again took his place. As the music changed, the celebrant asked the congregation to stand for the bride. Michelle was radiant in a soft, ivory chiffon dress. Escorted by her sister, Alice, who was also giving Michelle away.

The crowd was seated as they read their vows. The celebrant read softly from her program and asked for the rings. Davis looked at George, who looked at Stuart, who looked at Billy. The crowd laughed as Billy took off his shoe and pulled both rings out of his sock. He gave them to Stuart, who gave them to George, who passed them to Davis.

"You may now kiss the bride", the celebrant said. The crowd cheered and whistled as Davis bent Michelle down in a romantic dip.

Sipping on her wine, Claire toasted her glass as Uncle George held his glass up for the bride and groom. Dinner was delicious and everyone seemed to be having a wonderful time. As Dad and Michelle danced their first dance, Claire sat feeling completely content. She was happy, happier than she had felt in a long time, but tinged with sadness that she was going to have to say goodbye to the first man she ever loved sooner rather than later. A sharp stab of grief suddenly hit her hard in the chest and the sting of tears touched her eyes when a hand appeared in front of her.

"May I have this dance, pretty girl?"

She looked up into his soulful blue eyes, his gaze gave her goosebumps as she took his hand and was led out on the dance floor. The music was slow and romantic, she rested her head on his shoulder as he swayed gently.

"Did I tell you how beautiful you look tonight?" He looked down into her teary eyes and gently lowered his lips to hers and kissed her gently.

"May I cut in?" Davis said, tapping Stuart on the arm. Stuart smiled and took Michelle for a spin around the dancefloor. Claire wrapped her arms around Dad's neck and smiled.

"How are you going, Daddy?"

Davis smiled and dipped his daughter down and back up laughing.

"Thank you for everything, Claire, I know you and Amy have worked hard to make today happen, I'm so proud of you".

She could feel that sting of tears coming again. "I love you Daddy", she whispered in his ear, resting her cheek on his shoulder as they slow danced.

"He loves you darlin', he told me", Davis said quietly as Claire lifted her head to gaze over his shoulder, watching Stuart dance with Amy now. "I hope he makes you happy, the only thing I wish for is my girls to be happy".

Claire smiled at her father and kissed him on the cheek.

"I am happy, Daddy".

Michelle threw her bouquet and Amy caught it. She sat quietly with Tim when she stood up and tapped her glass.

"I'd like everyone to raise their glasses now that we are coming to the end of a beautiful night, I'd like to thank my big sister, Claire, for helping create this magical evening", she said as everyone clapped loudly for Claire who stood up and took a bow. "Tonight, after talking to my dad, I'd like to announce that Tim and I are having a baby". She bent down and kissed Tim as a loud whistle and cheers rang through the reception. "I didn't want to steal the show tonight, but Dad assured me he couldn't imagine a more special way to end the night, please raise your glasses and toast one last time to the bride and groom as they head off tonight to Hamilton Island for a week in the sun".

Claire wrapped her arms around her sister and hugged her tighter than ever before, she kissed Tim on the cheek in congratulations.

"Why didn't you tell me?". Claire put her hand on her little sister's belly. "Oh my god, I can feel a lil bump", Claire said as Stuart handed her a fresh glass of wine.

Claire and all the guests gathered when Michelle came down the front stairs in a beautiful red dress. Davis and Michelle were heading to Reffshore for the night and then flying out to the Whitsundays the next day. Dad didn't want to wait, he wanted to enjoy every moment he could as a married man before he wouldn't be able to anymore.

Stuart took Claire by the hand, and they walked back down the drive to the Grove Cottage. It was midnight and most of the guests had gone except for those handful of family who were still drinking and dancing.

"Close your eyes, pretty girl". She smiled softly and did as she was told. He opened the door and led her into the loungeroom. "Ok, you can open".

Claire opened her eyes and instantly a chill ran down her spine, there were rose petals leading a pathway across the lounge and down the hallway. He took her hand and led her down the hall, following the rose petal path before stopping at the bedroom. Stuart took her hand and kissed her fingers as he pushed the door open to a deep, incandescent glow. There were candles on every piece of furniture and the windowsill, there were hundreds of them, tea light, tall pillar candles, small, scented ones, and on the dresser was a vase with red roses and red candles around it.

Her eyes filled with tears as he kissed her, cupping her face in his hands.

"I love you, Claire", he said quietly. He lifted her off her feet and placed her gently on the bed.

"I love you too".

Chapter 16

The rain had fallen really heavily during the night and the clouds were low and still a deep grey. Stuart looked out the kitchen window at the water pooling on the drive as Claire put her shoes on and picked up her bag ready to go into Reffshore central for her first day of teaching.

"I don't think we will achieve much today in this weather", Billy said, dreading the thought of sitting in the tractor for hours.

"Might just drench the steers from Ruby Row, Bill, the vet from Reffshore is coming out to look at that one with the abscess".

"Do I look ok?" She asked the room as she looked in the sideboard mirror and straightened her jacket.

"Perfect, you will knock 'em dead", Billy said as he drank the last of his coffee.

"I don't think I've ever been so terrified". Laughing nervously as she kissed Stuart goodbye. "I'll see you this afternoon". Stuart stood on the verandah and watched as her little blue car disappeared down the drive into the foggy drizzle.

Bill pulled on his boots and coat, dreading going outside. Davis was due back from his honeymoon today and Stuart wanted to make sure the last of the drenching was done before he got home. There had been rain over the last few nights, so the ground was muddy and, in some parts, flooded with water. Jamie and Terry went out on the farm bikes after Claire left and bought the Ruby Row cattle into the yards by mid-morning. Going through in groups of ten at a time, they headed down the race, one by one, onto the scales. Terry pushed the button to register their weight before pushing them gently down to Stuart who put the tube into their mouths and pulled the nozzle trigger that gave them the dose required, sending them out the other end to Billy and Jamie who then sent them out through to another yard. The rest were healthy Black Angus. As Stuart finished, Billy counted 59 before opening the gates to the grazing paddock near the Grove Cottage.

"Leave them in there, Bill, for a few weeks, the grass is getting a bit long, it will save me slashing". Stuart said as a ute pulled up beside the yards. A young man in khaki overalls got out carrying his kit.

"G-day Darcy", Stuart said, shaking his hand as he led the vet into the yard.

The steer he had come to see had a big abscess which protruded profoundly from his neck. It would have been the size of a small rockmelon. Abscesses were something they had every now and then, but this one was definitely on the larger side. Stuart and Darcy pushed him gently into the crush.

"It's a ripper this one", Darcy chuffed as he felt the steer's neck. "My guess would be a grass seed in there has festered".

He took out his clippers and shaved the hair away from one side and gave the area a local.

"Been busy, Darce?"

"Yeah mate, it's been pretty full-on this week, got a few with Campylobacter over at the Sommer's place", he replied as he wiped antibacterial solution on the skin before opening the scalpel and cutting a small hole in the side of the abscess, sending neon yellow fluid and pus all over the ground. He massaged the abscess and sent lumps the size of grapes spilling out. After he washed it out and packed and sprayed the wound, he gave the steer a few shots of antibiotics.

"I'd leave him in the yards for a few days and let that drain more, I'll come back later in the week and check it", Darcy said as he and Stuart walked back to his ute.

"When is Davis due back?"

"This arvo sometime, mate".

"Pass on my regards".

"No worries. I'll see you later in the week". Stuart said as he left.

Davis and Michelle got home late in the afternoon. It was starting to drizzle again when Stuart helped them carry their bags into the house.

"Thanks, Tony", Davis said to Stuart as he shut the door behind them. Michelle looked seriously at Stuart when suddenly Davis slumped down onto the floor holding his head. Michelle raced to his side and touched his cheek.

"Davis, Davis, can you hear me?" she asked loudly as he stared at her with vacant eyes. Stuart called an ambulance while Michelle rolled him over onto his side in the recovery position, pulling the throw from the lounge and placing it over him to keep him warm.

Stuart was pacing up and down the verandah when he heard a car coming up the driveway. It was Claire. The sound of sirens were becoming louder in the distance and Claire looked horrified as the ambulance pulled in behind her. She skidded her little blue sedan to a grinding halt, running towards the house without even turning the car off.

"What's going on?" Claire screamed.

Stuart tried to stop her, but she burst through the door to see Michelle cradling Dad's head in her lap.

"Daddy", she shrieked as the two ambulance officers came into the room after her. Stuart pulled her away as she cried loudly.

The ambulance officers called out to Davis loudly while they assessed him. An oxygen mask was put on and various machines connected to him by wires and sticky dots on the chest.

"Is he ok? Daddy, Daddy can you hear me?" Claire yelled from across the room as Billy came rushing up to the house after seeing the ambulance pull up. Claire was wailing and yelling across to room to her father.

"Come on, Claire, come outside", Billy said, putting his arm around her and leading her out of the room.

It was 20 minutes later when the officer came out to the van to bring the stretcher for Davis to be transported to hospital.

"Is my father ok?", Claire asked, desperately needing answers.

"He is stable but he will need to go to hospital, maybe you could grab him some toiletries and have Bill take you into Reffshore and meet us there, you could let them know we are coming", the officer said to Claire, trying to give her a job to do to keep her occupied, even though, from regular updates, the hospital already knew the situation, he knew she needed to do something.

Davis was wheeled out not long after with Michelle and Stuart following. He was loaded into the van and the officer let Michelle come in the ambulance with them.

"I will call Amy and George and follow you in shortly", Stuart said giving her a gentle hug.

Amy and Tim came into the waiting area to see Claire and Stuart sitting on the far side beside the coke machine. It had been 3 hours since Davis was bought in via ambulance. Billy headed back to *November* to answer phone calls and finish some jobs. Amy sat down next to Claire. There wasn't much Claire could say other than to relay what had happened at home.

"Dad called Stuart, Tony, that's strange". Amy was too upset to think clearly about what was happening.

"The doctor said, when Dad got the results, that we would start to see symptoms like memory loss and confusion. Michelle said he had been having a few headaches during the week and that also is something that was on the list of possible symptoms". Claire put her hand on Amy's stomach. "Try not to stress too much".

Amy sat for a while, changed position twice and then crossed her legs on the chair.

"Seriously how long does it take", Amy said, standing up and pacing the room. Tim reached for her hand and pulled her onto his lap. "You work here, can't you go and see what is taking so long?" Tim nodded and walked over to the window to talk to the triage nurse.

"I am sure they will come out and get us as soon as there is any news, Amy". Claire was getting more and more annoyed by the moment, not at waiting, but at her sister's fidgeting. Tim walked back and sat next to Amy.

"She really doesn't know much but she said she will give Michelle a message and see if she can pop out to see you".

Stuart put his arm around Claire, and she rested her head on his shoulder and sighed deeply. Claire stared at the waiting room clock, 9.35pm. The emergency dept door opened and Michelle came out. She was met by Amy who caught her in a hug before she got to sit down.

"What's going on?" Claire asked.

Michelle reached into her bag and opened the water she was drinking and took a few mouthfuls.

"They are doing some scans and blood tests, but they are pretty sure that the bigger of the tumours in his brain is what is causing the problem, I don't know the technical terms for it all".

"Can we go in and see him? Is he awake?" Amy asked sternly. Michelle took Amy's hand and looked right into her eyes.

"He is unconscious," Michelle said calmly. "The doctor said just you girls can come in, I'm sorry, Stuart, but that's all they will allow for now".

Stuart didn't look surprised and he wasn't offended at all, but he was worried about Claire and how she was going to take seeing her father this way. He was given up to three months, and only a month had passed so far. Stuart felt, in his heart, as he watched her walk through those doors, that Davis would not be the same now and it scared him. This was a strong, cheeky man who had been his best mate most of their lives, who was now so sick. The end was coming, and the only thing Stuart could think about, and be thankful for, was that he had that chance when he did to ask for Claire's hand.

Amy and Claire followed Michelle down the emergency room corridor to one of the rooms across from the nurse's station with blue curtains drawn. It was very quiet, and Claire took a deep breath as she followed her sister through the gap in the curtain. Amy was sobbing quietly as she almost ran to Dad's side, taking his hand and sitting beside him. He was propped up on a few pillows with an oxygen mask on. He looked much older, and Claire stood at the end of the bed fighting the urge to cry. Not long after they came in, a nurse, a tall red headed woman doctor, and Dr Wong came and pulled the curtain closed behind them. The young doctor took his chart for a debriefing.

"Hi there, I am Dr Harding, and of course, you know Dr Wong, I'm one of the residents here," she addressed Dr Wong during her run down. "Mr Gannon collapsed at home this afternoon resulting in him being ambulanced here at 6.12pm, since then he has had an MRI which you have already read over", she sat down on the end of the empty bed beside Davis. Dr Wong opened a folder and read over his notes.

"The MRI shows a significant bleed of the larger of the lesions in the brain which has caused another stroke, I'm afraid". Dr Wong wrote a few notes down as he looked at the monitor. "Oxygen and pain relief is all we can offer now".

"Will you put him on a life support?" Michelle asked. Dr Wong looked critically at Michelle then ruffled through his folder of notes and handed her a document. Michelle went pale and looked up at Amy, her eyes filled with tears as she passed it to Claire.

"What is that?" Amy asked.

"Are you serious, a DNR?" Claire exclaimed. "When did he sign this?" Claire demanded.

"Michelle is his wife now; can't she change this?" Amy asked as she looked at Dr Wong, his eyes fell to the ground.

"I'm afraid not, Davis came to my office a few days after you were both here for the last set of scan results, he made it very clear to me that this is what he wanted".

"That selfish bastard. So, what, we just sit here now and let him slowly die?" Amy yelled as she stormed from the room.

Claire handed the DNR back to Dr Wong. Claire knew why he did it. He wanted to go on his own terms, she understood that more than most. Dad was the one who had to make the decision to turn off Mum's life support, she knew that he didn't want to burden them with that decision, so he just took it out of their hands.

"Did he discuss with you what his wishes were when this time came?"

"Are you saying he won't ever wake up now?" Claire asked incredulously. "He was walking around six hours ago; how can this be happening?" She burst out, folding her arms. The frustration was starting to set in.

"We discussed it briefly; he was pretty adamant that he didn't want to die at home when the time came". Michelle tried to search her memories for anything else Davis may have said but just couldn't remember. "I looked into the palliative care unit here for their help at home before the wedding, but I never thought it would happen this quickly, so I didn't finish the paperwork yet, I thought he'd have more time, I just thought he would have more time", she whispered.

Dr Wong was helpful in organising a meeting with palliative care and he was determined to get him a bed at a facility at Reffshore. Davis was in the final stages of his fight now.

A few days later, Dad was moved into the Reffshore's, Franklin House Hospice. He was still unconscious but had a room that faced the gardens. Michelle bought a few boxes of his favourite things from home, she set up photos around the room and on his bedside table.

Dad was on oxygen and was breathing noisily. He lay in the bed with the tv on the sports channel as that is something he liked to watch. Claire sat in the recliner at the side of his bed, watching his chest move up and down. Michelle pottered around the room talking to Dad like she would any other time, about the weather and the terrible food the hospital café had.

"Do you think he could still just wake up?" Claire asked quietly. Michelle stopped fussing with his blankets and looked up at her with hurt in her eyes and smiled.

"I guess we just have to stay positive, I hope he can hear us, that's why I keep talking to him".

Michelle took the empty jug off the table and left the room for some ice. Claire watched her leave before standing up and taking a seat on the bed beside Dad.

"Daddy, if you can hear me, open your eyes". She said taking his hand. "I need to talk to you, I have so many things I still need to tell you, but I need you to open your eyes and let me know you can hear me". She said as tears started to build, and her voice began to croak. "Do you remember that day when Amy fell off the tool shed roof and broke her arm?" She looked up at the ceiling trying not to cry. "I think she was seven, Billy and I were playing, and I told her she couldn't play and to leave us alone and I slammed the door on her." Claire wiped a tear as it fell down her cheek. "She was up there trying to look in the window at our game when she fell, it was my fault she broke her arm". Claire admitted.

Michelle opened the door quietly and put the jug of icy water on the table between the recliners as Claire wiped her eyes.

"You should go home and have a shower. I will stay with him. I promise I will call you if there is any change", Michelle said giving Claire a long tight hug.

"I guess I could freshen up a bit". Claire kissed Michelle on the cheek and walked to the door, she looked back at Dad for a moment before closing the door behind her.

Claire sat at the table in the kitchen, late in the day, eating a bowl of cornflakes. Staring off into space, she was startled by Stuart as he came in for a coffee.

"Hey there, pretty girl", he said as he leant down and kissed her gently. Claire didn't say anything, she stood up and wrapped her arms around his neck.

"Come on", he said as he took her hand and led her down the hallway, opening the bathroom door for her. The room was dimly lit with several candles along the windowsill, the bath water steamed, and bubbles glistened like crystals in the candlelight. "I thought you could use some time to relax", he whispered. Claire kissed him softly.

"Maybe you could join me", she said as she unbuttoned his shirt.

Chapter 17

Claire woke in Stuart's arms the next morning. It was early and the rising sunlight was starting to fill the room. She looked across to see him looking at her and, lost in his eyes, she forgot about her dad for a while.

"Good morning, pretty girl", he said softly as he kissed her nose. She smiled and rolled over, so she was sitting across his hips. Stuart reached his hands up into her hair and pulled her into a deep kiss. She was naked and her tanned skin prickled with goosebumps as he ran his fingers up her back and she released a deep moan. He raised his lips to kiss her neck before flipping her over onto her stomach, kissing all the way down her back sending another flutter of goosebumps across her skin. He made love to her that morning like it was the first time. He groaned deeply as she arched her back up towards his chest, she could feel him tremble as he came. It was hot and quick. They had not had much time alone together in the last weeks and she missed him terribly.

"I love you, Stuart", she whispered as they lay together. Stuart felt suddenly emotional and, in that moment, he knew it was the right time, he reached over into the top draw beside the bed and pulled out a small red box. Claire looked at the box in his hand and sat up quickly looking at him wide eyed.

"I asked your dad not long ago, it was important to me to have his blessing when it came time to ask, he gave me this for when the time came". Claire started to cry as Stuart opened the box to reveal her mother's engagement ring.

"I want to spend every day for the rest of my life falling deeper in love with you and I want to show you how much you mean to me every day for the rest of yours. Marry me, pretty girl?".

Claire wrapped her arms around his neck crying.

"I can't believe you asked Dad, yes". She said as he took the ring from the box and slid it on her finger.

Uncle George was sitting beside Dad's bed when Claire opened his room door. He gave her a cuddle and an affectionate kiss on the cheek before sitting back down holding his brother's hand. Claire could feel the happiness of Stuart's proposal being sucked out of her like a tornado funnel. Her eyes were itchy and sore, it felt like she couldn't cry anymore, but on the other side of that, she wanted to howl like a baby. "How has he been?"

"No change, love, he is peaceful". Michelle said as she hugged Claire tightly. Claire put her arm on Uncle George's shoulder, and he rubbed her hand.

"I guess we knew this time was going to come", he said, not taking his eyes off his brother. "The doctor said that they would just keep him comfortable now".

Uncle George had several books with him and looked to be settling in for the long haul. Claire sat on the edge of the bed looking at Dad. He was laying on his side with pillows propped up against his back. The nurse came in a few times since she arrived to check him. She spoke to him like he was awake to answer her. Telling him that it was a lovely day outside and that dinner that evening was a roast lamb and veg. Claire admired her and how she spoke to him, as she finished, she caught her in the hallway to thank her.

Come lunchtime, Dad's room was filled, everyone was there to have lunch with him. Stuart and the boys talked to him about the jobs that needed doing, the abscess on the steer's neck was healed, that they had 15ml of rain overnight. There was no awkwardness, just keeping it as normal as possible. A nurse was unfolding some towels as Amy was telling everyone that she could feel the baby move and pressed Dad's hand onto her belly so he could feel it too, before telling him that Claire, Tim, and herself were leaving to go to have an ultrasound while the nurses washed him.

"We'll be back in a few hours, Dad", Amy said picking up her bag and kissing him on the cheek.

As the day drifted on, the hours felt like days themselves. Michelle had been sitting quietly watching Davis's chest rise and fall. His breathing was no longer a noisy rattle. It was slow and steady. Uncle George sat reading his book as Dr Harding came in for the afternoon rounds. She touched Davis on the cheek affectionately and took his hand felt for his pulse before she wrote on his chart that was resting in her lap. She quietly walked across to the table and chairs in the corner of the room, sitting down next to Michelle.

"I think it's time to call the girls back". Dr Harding said touching her shoulder in comfort. Uncle George stood up quickly and took his mobile out into the hallway after hearing what the doctor said.

Michelle nodded. She had been watching his breathing over the day and she could see him slowing down.

"Is there anything I can get for you; anyone I can call?". Michelle shook her head, pressing a folded tissue to her face to absorb the tears.

"No, thank you for all that you have done for him, we all appreciate it". Michelle had been in this position before when her first husband died, the pain now was still as sharp as it was back then.

Dr Harding walked across to Davis and touched his arm again gently, in a sign of respect, and then left the room.

One at a time, the girls spent time alone with Davis. There were candles burning and Amy played Dad's favourite music. Davis lay on his back now. Claire quietly walked into the room after Michelle and Amy's turns. She took off her shoes and snuggled herself onto the bed beside her father, resting her head on his chest. She could hear a slow deep thud of his heart beating. It was the greatest sound in the world. Looking up into his peaceful face she kissed him on the cheek gently as her tears fell onto his skin.

"I don't want to say goodbye". Claire cried hard. She wanted to disappear, to run away. "I love you, Daddy, thank you for giving your blessing to Stuart, he told me he asked you for my hand". Claire took Dad's hand and moved his fingers over her hand so he could feel the ring on her finger. "He asked, Daddy, and I said yes, I wish you could be there to walk me down the aisle". She rested her head back on his chest listening to his heartbeat.

Amy, Michelle, and Uncle George came back in not long after. Uncle George sat on the end of his bed, Claire didn't move, her head still resting on his chest and her eyes closed. Michelle and Amy sat quietly beside him. Michelle rested her head on his other shoulder and Amy held his hand. Davis took a quick deep breath and slowly exhaled. Amy felt his hand relax, she stood slowly beside the bed placing his hand on her belly for one last time and, just like the baby sensed it, it started kicking under his hand.

Claire listened to his heartbeat become slow and distant until she couldn't hear it anymore. She opened her tear-filled eyes looking directly across Dad's chest to Michelle who nodded softly. Amy was still holding his hand to her belly as she started to sob loudly. Claire lifted her head to look at Dad's face. He was gone, she knew he was gone, but he looked like he was sleeping, only now, he looked calmer, no noise, just silence. George stood, leaned over to push the red button on the bedhead for the nurse. Life wouldn't change, as long as she stayed there, her head on his chest, in the silence, in that exact spot, she was still Daddy's girl for another few moments.

Time seemed to go so fast after that. Nurses rushing around fixing Davis ready for the funeral home to pick him up. Michelle, Claire, Amy, and Uncle George sat quietly in the room while the nurses worked. Dr Harding arranged his hands neatly on his chest and spread the sheet out over him, placing a flower in his hands. Stuart and Billy arrived, Dr Wong had come and signed his death certificate. He offered his sympathies before leaving quickly for another patient. Stuart stood beside his oldest friend.

"My friend," he said as he swallowed hard, resting his hand on Davis's chest. Stuart felt like a part of him had broken and he didn't know how to fix it, that sudden angst of pain that radiated through his body as he looked down at Davis was intense. Billy was a crying mess and was helped from the room by Michelle.

Claire stood beside Stuart and held his hand as they both looked at Dad. He turned to her, pulling her into his arms as a knock came on the door. Amy opened the door to find the funeral directors with a stretcher ready to take him. As they all left, one by one, Claire bent down and kissed her father for the last time on the cheek. It wasn't long before the funeral directors wheeled Davis out, he was covered in a lovely blue velvet sheet and loaded into the back of the van. Claire stood there until the car was out of sight. The sudden emptiness that engulfed her body was heavier than she could ever imagine.

Chapter 18

It was late afternoon, Amy and Claire sat in the examination room in the maternity ward. Amy lay on the bed with a trace monitor strapped around her belly. Claire watched the midwife's face as the small strip of paper fed out of the machine. She tore the sheet off and pinned it under her chart on the end of the bed as she put on a fresh set of gloves and proceeded to check Amy's cervix.

"You are three centimetres, my dear, this little bub is on the way, your trace read is showing some minor contractions". Amy looked nervous.

"I suggest you head home and try to get some rest, if you want to, you can walk to help things move along faster, but for now I am afraid it's a waiting game, when your contractions are ten minutes apart, come back in".

Amy didn't seem uncomfortable as Claire drove her back to Tim's house. It was close to the hospital so, if needed, she could get help quickly. Amy had been spending a lot of time at *November* in the last 4 months since Dad died, helping clean and go through his things. Davis had left a very detailed Will, he wanted some of his belongings given to selected people and the girls had spent quite some time making sure his wishes were completed. Tim rubbed Amy's back as she leant down on the kitchen bench as a contraction came and went quickly.

"I will duck home, have a shower and get a change of clothes and come back soon, it's going to be a long night

I'd say". Claire kissed her sister on the cheek, touched her chest and then Amy's. "I, you".

Amy smiled and touched her chest and then back at Claire.

"Look after her," Claire said to Tim, and she went to the door.

"She is in the right hands" Tim said proudly flashing his doctor's winning grin.

Claire pulled off the main highway just as the sun sprayed its last rays of golden light for the day through the trees. She decided to take a back road, past Grinner Falls, home. She knew it was a faster way as her and Stuart had driven it many times, she was anxious and felt more and more desperate to get back to Amy, she tuned the first corner and sent dust flying high behind her.

Claire felt her skin prickle with good bumps as the gentle smell of lavender drifted past her. Claire closed her eyes for what she thought was the smallest moment, breathing in her mother. In that small gap of time, the world seemed to slow down, Claire had drifted onto the side of the dirt road. When she opened her eyes, it was too late to react. The ute slid down the side of the embankment ripping several small pine saplings on the roadside out by the roots. The ute hit a large fallen tree trunk hard, the windscreen shattered as it rolled twice, coming to rest on the driver's side at the bottom of the incline, then there was silence. Steam escaped from under the crushed bonnet, the headlights lit the surrounding bush as the sun completely went down. The debris slowly settled, and the air became clear.

It was 8pm. The house phone at *November* rang several times and went to messenger. The house was dark, the power was out. Michelle fumbled her way around in the dark looking for the phone that was ringing again.

"Hello", she said finally.

"Hey, Michelle, its Tim, I was hoping to talk to Claire", Michelle was confused, she placed the phone on her shoulder and struck a match to light some candles.

"I thought she was with you guys; she isn't here, love".

Tim told Michelle that Claire said she was heading home, but that was over three hours ago, and he thought she would have been back by now.

"I'll call Stuart on his mobile; she might be with him". Tim hung up the phone and dialled Stuart's number just as his ute pulled into Tim's Drive. The panic started to set in when Tim stepped outside, and Stuart walked up to the porch.

"Is Claire with you?" Tim asked holding the phone tightly.

"No, I thought she was here, I bought some dinner for you all from Michelle, there is a black out at *November* so she sent it in to heat up for everyone". Stuart read the concern on Tim's face as he handed the casserole dishes over to him.

"I'll head back out to Michelle; she may have turned up there". Stuart flicked the headlights on high beam and put his foot down. There was a heavy feeling filling his stomach. Where could she be? Has something happened to her?

Claire opened her eyes. It took her several minutes to realise where she was. She had drifted in and out of consciousness a few times over the last hour. She could see the headlights dimly lighting up the bush around her as she lay on her side against the door, looking out the crumpled hole where the windscreen had been. She lifted her hand and touched the side of her face, she could feel a deep cut on her head that was dribbling blood down the side of her cheek. The dash was firmly pushed against her. She couldn't move. She reached forward to the steering wheel and pushed the horn. There was no sound. She let out a loud scream as she tried to pull herself forward to feel around the dash. It was Dad's ute she was in, and he had bodgeed the dash with a selection of switches and buttons. She pushed the first three and nothing happened.

"Come on, Daddy, help me", she whispered as she reached forward again to flip a silver switch. The cars headlights suddenly seemed a lot brighter as the spotlight on the roof flickered into life. She hoped anyone coming along the road would see the lights...

At 10.30pm after several calls to friends and family, and with no sign of Claire, Michelle sat across from Stuart at the kitchen table and dialled the police. Stuart rang a few neighbours who all agreed to start looking for Claire. Within thirty minutes a local man, Wayne Frankston, and his two sons arrived. Stuart relayed the timeline since she was last seen.. Billy and Terry would go back along the town road looking for any signs of her. Wayne and his sons would take the road that went past the show ground also back into town.

Eddie, in the paddy wagon, drove the highway towards *November*. There were several ways to get to *November* from town. Most of those had been covered by searchers except one, and in his heart, he knew it was the way she went. Eddie pulled the paddy wagon off the highway down the winding dirt track near Grinners, it was nearly invisible from the main road. There was a lot of mud and debris, but he pushed on. He used the spotlight on the roof to light up the road like the Vegas Strip. After a few corners, he saw the heavy creases in the mud on the shoulder and the broken saplings where the ute left the road. He pulled the paddy wagon up on the edge, facing the spotlight down through the broken tree line and got out.

"Claire". He bellowed as loud as he could. He could see down the incline and the lights from the spotlight

Claire had managed to turn on. Without hesitation, Eddie started running down towards the light at the bottom.

"Claire", he yelled again, his shaky voice echoed through the bush like it was a deep walled cave. He reached the ute, sliding himself down into the gap where the windscreen met the bonnet. He reached forward as far as he could in the dim, dusty light and touched her face gently.

"Claire, it's Eddie, can you hear me?" Claire opened her eyes slowly. "Claire?"

"Eddie". She whispered.

Eddie sighed with relief to hear her voice. He reached onto his shoulder and pushed the button on his radio to call for help.

"I'm gonna get you out of here, Claire". Eddie desperately started pulling the debris from in front of the cab so he could get closer to her, the bonnet was bent at such an angle that he couldn't move it. He reached into the cab, pulling himself forward with the steering wheel, through a small gap, so his upper body was in with her. He felt around her looking for injuries which he was relaying back to the emergency services via radio. He took off his jacket and put it over her shoulders and held her hand.

"Stuart", she whispered softly between laboured breaths. Eddie pulled himself closer to her, reaching down to feel her legs. She was pinned heavily against the dash, her leg was broken, he could feel the bone poking through her jeans.

"He is coming, don't worry, it's going to be ok". Eddie said to reassure her as he pulled himself further into the wreckage trying to find a way to help her.

"Amy is having the baby, I need to go back to town, Mum is there, I don't know where she has gone, she said she would be back in a minute" Claire mumbled. She had a deep laceration on her forehead that was bleeding down her cheek, onto her neck. He listened to her breathing and gurgling as she slipped back into unconsciousness. The moment she mentioned her mother, his heart sank. He lay with his feet in the air, his upper body over the steering wheel holding her hand. He felt even more desperate to get her out, he didn't want to lose her, not after her mother.

Eddie heard a car pull to a sliding stop up on the road, and before long Billy had slid down the hill to see the wreckage. Billy launched himself onto the side of the cab, so he was looking through the passenger window down at Claire and face to face with Eddie.

"She is asking for Stuart" Eddie said to Billy in a desperate voice, he could see by the look on his face that the situation was not good. Billy pulled the phone from his pocket and dialled Stuart's number.

"You better tell him to hurry". Eddie said as he checked her pulse again.

Within half an hour, due to Eddie calling it in on the police radio, paramedics and the SES had arrived and moved them back up to the road forming a barricade of sorts. The SES had tall lights erected at the top of the hill. They had removed the buckled bonnet and were slowly cutting into the dash to free her legs. A paramedic had edged carefully into where Eddie had been and was prepping her to move and gave her some pain medication.

It wasn't long before Stuart slid his ute sideways in behind the ambulance to see Eddie on the road, his shirt covered in blood, standing with Billy and Wayne Frankston. He leapt from his ute and stood on the road looking down the incline to see the wreck. He threw himself down the rocky, debris covered slope with no concern for his own life. The female paramedic stopped him as he reached them.

"Claire", he yelled desperately trying to get past.

"Sir, Sir, you will need to wait up on the road", she said with her hands pushing on his chest. An SES officer came over to assist Stuart back up the incline to where Billy and Eddie were waiting. Billy tapped Stuart on the shoulder in a sign of comfort as he paced up and down the side of the road. A loud snap echoed through the many voices as the first half of the dash was detached from the cab and clearing the way into Claire through the broken windscreen.

The rescue workers worked quickly to remove the last section of dash and she was ready to move. The rescue team edged her out slowly and loaded her onto the stretcher before a group of four men carried her up the embankment.

"Claire" again Stuart yelled desperately, being held back by Billy as they walked her past him. Eddie stood beside Claire as they prepped her to load into the ambulance.

Claire opened her eyes as she was pushed onto the pad that held the stretcher in place. She lifted her hand and touched Eddie on the arm.

"Thankyou", she whispered.

Eddie swallowed the lump building in his throat.

Somewhere, buried amongst a decade of hating him, she realised that he had saved her life, it was time to forgive the man who killed her mother.

The fog set in to create a misty rain above the wreckage. Stuart took her hand, walking along beside her as they loaded her into the ambo, he never let it go. He gently kissed her forehead, holding her hand tightly as they drove away towards town. She mumbled to herself on the way, and he could hear that her ramblings included her mum, it was like she was talking to her.

Chapter 19

The doctors were amazed at how strong she was. She hobbled out of Reffshore hospital only 4 weeks later on crutches. After everything she had been through the night of the accident her only main injury, besides cuts and bruises, was a broken leg which was pinned into place during surgery. There was certainly someone watching over her that night.

The following January, Claire pulled her little blue car into the near empty carpark at Reffshore Central Highschool, turned off the engine and just sat for a moment. She smiled gently as she took out her key, loaded up her arms with a bag of paperwork and equipment. Getting out, and shutting the door, she stepped to the side of her car and pushed the lock button on the remote and began to walk across the carpark into one of her lifelong dreams.

It was the gentle breeze carrying the smell of lavender that brought a smile to her face. She knew she was doing what she was destined to do, it was the courage it took to step into that dream that had taken her so long to find. Her father would be proud and as she opened the door into her office, she could feel him around her.

Since coming back to *November,* she had found that the one thing she longed for the most, even though she couldn't see it until now was to be home, to have a family and to love. To love her life. It took losing her father and finding a sense of peace with the loss of her mother and forgiving Eddie to find home again.

Home was the trees, it was the soil, it was that smell of lavender that crept up on her often. Home wasn't just a building, it's everything that makes you feel warm inside. That warmth is love. Time is a gift and we never have enough of it. She spent nearly 10 years trying to find peace, moving from place to place trying so desperately to find it, but in the end, all she had to do was go home. That first day, scared and nervous, when she took the last turn in her little blue car between the tall safety of those entrance gums, little did she know that life could be this beautiful.

The rain had eased overnight, and a warm glow of sunlight broke through the clouds to unveil the morning. The land always looked greener after the rain.

Claire sat quietly in the room looking directly onto the front gardens of *November*. The crisp air was addictive and filled with a fresh scent of lavender. It had been several months since her accident and Claire, sipping a glass of champagne, absorbed the morning glow as the hairdresser pinned flowers into her hair. *November* was radiant as the sun bounced off the vine covered walls.

Claire stepped into her dress. A beautiful white gown covered with intricate beading and lace. Michelle pushed her mother's veil comb into her hair as she turned to look back at her one last time, she tucked the small fly away curl behind her ear.

Claire watched Amy from the windows walk through the gardens humming to herself, carrying little Davis, Billy standing by the door proudly waiting to hand her the bouquet when it was time.

There was a peculiar feeling in the air. One of peace. *November* was beautiful during the Spring. Flowers bloomed boldly and the trees spread their newly formed leaves wide across the lawns. Guests gathered again under the same gum tree where Davis had married Michelle.

Claire ran her finger over her mother's ring and took the familiar but important path. She took it firstly on her own the day she arrived, it was now lined with tall stately flower beds that she and Amy planted all those months ago. On each side of the path, the flowers reached, leaning out with brightly coloured blooms to touch her like soft fingers as she walked by.

One stone at a time, Billy lead her 27,28,29...she took the last step. Standing in her white gown, the train falling softly on the small white pebbles behind her, she read the words on the headstone.

A Mother's love, like an imperishable sun, cannot go out.

Although the stone now also bore her father's name.

Claire stood there in silence, reading the words again and again and she lightly pressed her fingers in the space between the names.

"I ....you... like an imperishable sun" she whispered as she touched her fingers to her chest and then back to the headstone.

Claire brushed away a single tear as she reached out and took Billy's arm, ready for him to walk her down the aisle. The sweet smell of lavender filling the air.

Glossary of terms

Ute- Farm vehicle (utility vehicle) with a tray.

Bodgeed- Amateur modification of an item to perform a task it is not designed for – also, a temporary fix of an item with materials on hand.

Pissed- Drunk, also,

Pissed off - angry at someone.

SES- State Emergency Service.

Pub- Tavern or Hotel.

DNR- Do Not Resuscitate.

Shindig- Party.

Soggy- wet and soft.

Catch wind of it- find out about a secret.

Party pooper- a person who usually goes home early from a party or chooses to not participate.

To Clock - hit someone or something.

Peg – to throw something with force, (usually at someone)

Smart arse- someone who is cheeky.

Looking green- hungover or sick.

The common – a paddock usually shared by a community to put livestock in.

Togs- bathing suit or swimwear.

Copper- policeman.

CWA- Country Women's Association- a support group for people in country areas.

Lazy Boy- a comfortable single sofa that reclines.

Piece of work- an unkind or unpleasant person.

Telling a yarn- story telling.

Old duck- common term in Australia for an elderly person.

Jammed- to place something somewhere with unnecessary force.

Counter meal- a meal served at the local pub.

Pub grub- food served at a pub.

Campylobacter- a disease found in breeding Ewes which causes abortion of the unborn lamb.

www.ingramcontent.com/pod-product-compliance
Lightning Source LLC
Chambersburg PA
CBHW070033120726
47909CB00003B/1138